710分

分

四级阅读单项技能突破

王烨　赵立洁　等　编

中国水利水电出版社
www.waterpub.com.cn

内 容 提 要

本书是根据《大学英语四级考试大纲》阅读理解部分考试内容的最新改革而编写的，内容新颖，主题突出，实用性强。

书中第一章是阅读能力考核解读，主要向大家说明大纲的基本要求，让考生复习时做到"有法可依"。第二章是阅读自我测评部分，通过这部分，读者可以清楚地知道自己的做题漏洞，方便以后做有针对性的练习。第三章是阅读解题技巧，详细地归纳了各种阅读技巧和解题策略。第四章为阅读实践演练，所选的题材和篇幅与四级考试阅读中的文章长短相似、难易程度相仿。

本书适用于参加大学英语四级考试的读者。

图书在版编目（CIP）数据

710分四级阅读单项技能突破 / 王烨等编. -- 北京
: 中国水利水电出版社，2010.1
ISBN 978-7-5084-7141-9

Ⅰ. ①7… Ⅱ. ①王… Ⅲ. ①英语－阅读教学－高等学校－水平考试－自学参考资料 Ⅳ. ①H319.4

中国版本图书馆CIP数据核字(2010)第003434号

书　　　名	**710分四级阅读单项技能突破**
作　　　者	王烨　赵立洁　等　编
出 版 发 行	中国水利水电出版社
	（北京市海淀区玉渊潭南路1号D座　100038）
	网址：www. waterpub. com. cn
	E - mail：sales@waterpub. com. cn
	电话：(010) 68367658（营销中心）
经　　　售	北京科水图书销售中心（零售）
	电话：(010) 88383994、63202643
	全国各地新华书店和相关出版物销售网点
排　　　版	贵艺图文设计中心
印　　　刷	北京市地矿印刷厂
规　　　格	145mm×210mm　32开本　6.25印张　207千字
版　　　次	2010年1月第1版　　2010年1月第1次印刷
印　　　数	0001—5000册
定　　　价	**15.80元**

Preface
前　言

　　自从大学英语四六级考试改革以后，阅读理解部分的变动很大。改革后的阅读理解包括仔细阅读（Reading in Depth）和快速阅读（Skimming and Scanning），测试学生通过阅读获取书面信息的能力；所占分值比例为 35%，其中仔细阅读部分 25%，快速阅读部分 10%。考试时间 40 分钟。

　　首先是快速阅读部分采用 1～2 篇较长篇幅的文章或多篇短文，总长度约为 1000 个单词。要求考生运用略读和查读的技能从篇章中获取信息。略读考核学生通过快速阅读获取文章主旨大意或中心思想的能力，阅读速度为每分钟 100 个单词。查读考核学生利用各种提示，如数字、大写单词、段首或句首词等，快速查找特定信息的能力。快速阅读理解部分采用的题型有是非判断、句子填空、完成句子等。

　　仔细阅读部分要求考生阅读三篇短文。两篇为多项选择题型的短文理解测试，每篇长度为 300～350 个单词。一篇为选词填空（Banked Cloze）或简答题（Short Answer Questions），选词填空篇章长度为 200～250 个单词，简答题篇章长度为 300～350 个单词。仔细阅读部分测试考生在不同层面上的阅读理解能力，包括理解主旨大意和重要细节、综合分析、推测判断以及根据上下文推测词意等。多项选择题型的短文后有若干个问题，考生根据对文章的理解，从每题的 4 个选项中选择最佳答案。选词填空测试考生对篇章语境中的词汇理解和运用能力。要求考生阅读一遍删去若干词汇的短文，然后从所给选项中选择正确的词汇填空，使短文复原。简答题的篇章后有若干个问题，要求考生根据对文章的理解用最简短的表述（少于 10 个单词）回答问题或完成句子。

本书秉承"内容创新、能力创新"的原则，在编写逻辑上遵循"测与评·教与学·练与模"的思路，让考生在备考前准确抓住重点、难点和弱点，有针对性地进行复习。

"测与评"先让考生熟悉考试内容与结构，同时检测自身的英语水平，给自己一个比较准确的定位。"教与学"主要讲解大学英语四级考试的重点和应试技巧，考生可根据自己的具体情况学习其中的方法技巧。在"练与模"这一全书重要环节中，精选"应试难度"和"拔高难度"两个梯次的习题，进行考前热身，以达到让考生轻松应对考试的效果。

要想攻破"阅读"这个难关，必须通过认真的学习和足够的练习。本书正是按照这一标准进行编写的，相信读者通过本书的细致讲解和有针对性的练习，定能在考试中超常发挥，取得理想成绩！

本书由王烨、梁媛编写，马云秀、王建军、王海娜、王越、白云飞、刘梅、张世华、张红燕、张娟娟、张静、李光全、李良、李翔、李楚、陈仕奇、罗勇军、姜文琪、董敏、蒋卫华等同志也参与本书的编写工作，在此一并向他们表示感谢。

Contents

目　录

第一章 CET-4阅读能力考核解读

大学英语教学大纲是对本科英语教学的指导，大纲对阅读能力的基本要求是：能顺利阅读语言难度中等的一般性题材的文章，掌握中心大意以及说明中心大意的事实和细节，并能进行一定的分析、推理和判断，领会作者的观点和态度，阅读速度达到每分钟70个单词。在阅读篇幅较长、难度略低、生词不超过总词数3%的材料时，能掌握中心大意，捉住主要事实和有关细节，阅读速度达到每分钟100个单词。

阅读理解能力测试的主要方面：

（1）读材料的主旨和大意，以及用以说明主旨和大意的事实和细节。

（2）既理解具体的事实，也理解抽象的概念。

（3）既理解字面的意思，也理解深层的含义，包括作者的态度，意图等。

（4）既理解某句，某段的含义，也理解全篇的逻辑关系，并据此进行推理和判断。

（5）既能根据所提供的信息去理解，也能结合大学生应有的常识去理解。

根据这5项要求，我们可将阅读理解多项选择题归纳为以下几种题型：细节理解题，词句理解题，主题、主旨题，猜测词意题，推理判断题。

大学英语四级考试是全面考核结束基础阶段英语学习的学生是否达到教学大纲所规定的各项目标。以下为大学英语四级考试中的阅读考试内容介绍：

四级考试包括5个部分，第二大题阅读理解共20题，总分为40分，即每道题2分。考试时间35分钟。

阅读理解题要求考生阅读4篇短文，总阅读量不超过1000个单词。每篇短文后有5个问题。考生应根据文章内容从每题4个选择项中选出一个最佳答案。

一、阅读理解选材的原则

（1）题材广泛，可以包括人物传记、社会、文化、日常知识、科普常识等，但是所涉及的背景知识应能为学生所理解。

（2）体裁多样，可以包括叙述文、说明文、议论文等。

（3）文章的语言难度中等，无法猜测而又影响理解的关键词，如超出大学英语教学大纲四级词汇表的范围，用汉语注明词意。

二、阅读理解部分主要测试的能力

（1）掌握所读材料的主旨和大意。

（2）了解和说明主旨和大意的事实和细节。

（3）既理解字面的意思，也能根据所读材料进行一定的判断和推论。

（4）既理解个别句子的意义，也理解上下文的逻辑关系。

阅读理解部分的目的是测试学生通过阅读获取信息的能力，既要求准确，也要求有一定的速度。

三、阅读理解技能概述

大学英语教学大纲中列出的语言技能表中的阅读技能为理解主题和中心思想（Understanding the Topic and Main Idea）。阅读的首要目的是看懂所读材料的主旨大意。

辨认主题句是获取文章主旨大意的一个有效方法。主题句的特点为结构一般比较简单，表述的意思比较概括。

　　有些文章首尾都有主题句前后呼应，两次点题。对于没有主题句的文章，可把文中细节所集中论述的要点，运用逻辑推理的方法，酝酿出文章的主题。抓住了文章的中心思想，也就不难用浓缩、简练的语言，概括出文章的标题。

第二章 CET-4 阅读自我测评

第一节 快速阅读测与评

▶**Passage one**

Reading Comprehension (Skimming and Scanning) (15 minutes)

Directions: *In this part, you will have 15 minutes to go over the passage quickly and answer the questions on Answer Sheet 1.*

For questions 1-7, mark

Y (*for YES*)　　　　　*if the statement agrees with the information given in the passage;*

N (*for NO*)　　　　　*if the statement contradicts the information given in the passage;*

NG (*for NOT GIVEN*)　*if the information is not given in the passage.*

For questions 8-10, complete the sentences with the information given in the passage.

Theft Deterrent System

To deter the vehicle theft, the system is designed to give an alarm and keep the engine from being started if any of the front, sliding and back doors and hood is forcibly unlocked or the battery terminal is disconnected and then reconnected when the vehicle is locked. The alarm blows the horn intermittently and flashes the headlights, tail lights and other exterior lights. The engine cannot be started because the starter circuit will be cut.

Setting the System

1. Turn the ignition key to the "LOCK" position and remove it.

2. Have all passengers get out of the vehicle.

3. Close and lock the front, sliding and back doors and hood.

The indicator light will come on when the front, sliding and back doors and hood are closed and locked. As the front doors are locked, the system will give you a preparation time of 30 seconds before the setting, during which the front, sliding and back doors and hood may be opened to prepare for the setting.

Be careful not to use the key when opening either front door. This will cancel the system.

4. After making sure the indicator light starts flashing, you may leave the vehicle. The system will automatically be set after the preparation time elapses. The indicator light will flash to show the system is set. If any of the front, sliding and back doors and hood is opened at that time, the setting is interrupted until it is closed and locked. Never leave anyone in the vehicle when you set the system, because unlocking from the inside will activate (使启动) the system.

When the System is Set

Activating the system. The system will give the alarm and cut the starter circuit under the following conditions:

If any of the front, sliding and back doors and hood is unlocked without using the key.

If the battery terminal is disconnected and then reconnected.

After one minute, the alarm will automatically stop with the starter circuit cut kept on.

Reactivating the alarm

Once set, the system automatically resets the alarm each time the front, sliding and back doors and hood are closed after the alarm stops.

The alarm will be activated again under the following conditions:

If any of the front, sliding and back doors and hood is opened. If the battery terminal is disconnected and then reconnected.

Stopping the alarm

Turn the ignition key from the "LOCK" to "ACC" position. The alarm will be stopped with the starter circuit cut kept on. Stopping the alarm in this manner will keep the alarm from being reactivated when any of the front, sliding and back doors and hood is opened.

Interrupting the setting

With the system set, the back door can be opened with the key without activating or canceling the system. While it is open, the front and sliding doors and hood may be opened in addition, and the system can be activated only by the battery terminal disconnection.

To resume the setting, close and lock the front, sliding and back doors and hood. The back door must be closed with the key removed.

Cancelling the System

Unlock either front door with the key, or unlock the sliding door with the key when it has been closed. This cancels the system completely and the starter circuit cut will be cancelled at once.

Indicator Light

The indicator light gives the following three indications when the system is in use. When the light is:

Flashing — The system is set. You need the key to open the front, sliding and back doors and hood.

On — The system will automatically be set when the time comes. The front, sliding and back doors and hood may be opened without a key.

Off — The system is inactive. You may open any door and hood.

Testing the System

1. Open the driver's and front passenger's windows.

2. Set the system as described above. The front doors should be locked with the key. Be sure to wait until the indicator light starts flashing.

3. Unlock one of the front, sliding and back doors from the inside. The system should activate the alarm.

4. Cancel the system by unlocking either front door with the key.

5. Repeat this operation for the other doors and hood. When testing

on the hood, also check that the system is activated when the battery terminal is disconnected and then reconnected.

If the system does not work properly, have it checked by your Toyota dealer.

提示：在实考试卷中，8~10 题在答题卡 1 上。

1. The system is used to deter the vehicle theft according to the instructions.

2. In order to set the system, you should have all passengers get out of the vehicle.

3. The system will be cancelled when you use the key to open the back door.

4. The system will be not be activated unless you use the key to open any of the front, sliding and back doors and hood.

5. In order to stop the alarm, you have to turn the ignition key from the "ACC" to "LOCK" position.

6. When the indicator light is flashing, it is needless to use the key to open any of the doors and hood.

7. The passage tells us that the system works so effectively that it never breaks down.

8. As the front doors are locked, the theft deterrent system will give you a preparation time of _____ before setting.

9. Before leaving the vehicle, make sure that the indicator light _____ _____.

10. According to the passage, if the system refuses to work properly, have it checked by your _____.

答案　1. Y 2. Y 3. N 4. N 5. N 6. N 7. NG
　　　8. 30 seconds 9. starts flashing 10. Toyota dealer

解析：

1. Y)。该句句意为：根据说明，该系统是用来防止车辆偷盗的。本题解题依据为文章第一段第一句话，与原文之意相符。

2. Y)。该句句意为：设定该防盗系统时，你应该让所有乘客下车。本题依据为 Setting the system 标题下列出的第二点，与原文之意吻合。

3. N)。该句句意为：当用钥匙打开车后门时，该系统设置将被取消。本题解题依据为 Cancelling the system 下面一段，该段大意为：用钥匙打开前门或滑门该系统将完全取消，显然本题句意与原文所述不符。

4. N)。该句句意为：该系统只有在使用钥匙打开前门、滑门、后门及发动机罩时才会启动。本题解题依据为 Activating the system 下面第二句话即 If any of the front, sliding and back doors and hood is unlocked without using the key （如不用钥匙打开前门、滑门、后门和发动机罩，该系统将发出警报并切断起动机电路），由此可见，该句意与本题之意相反。

5. N)。该句句意为：如果终止警报，你得把车的点火钥匙从 "ACC" 位置拨到 "LOCK" 位置。本题解题依据为 Stopping the alarm 下面第一句话：Turn the ignition key from the "LOCK" to "ACC" position （把点火钥匙从 "LOCK" 拨到 "ACC" 位置），显然与原文不符。

6. N)。该句句意为：当指示灯闪烁时，不需要用钥匙打开任何门和发动机罩。本题解题依据为 Indicator light 下面的第二句话：You need the key to open the front, sliding and back doors and hood. （你需要钥匙打开前后门、滑门和发动机罩）。显然本题句意与原文所述不符。

7. NG)。该句句意为：本文告诉我们该系统能有效工作以致于从未出现故障。通览全文，本文根本未提及该信息。因而无法得知。

8. 30 seconds 答案依据为本文 Setting the system 标题下 "... the system will give you a preparation time of 30 setting..."。

9. starts flashing 答案依据为 Setting the system 标题下，小标题 4 后面的内容。

10. Toyota dealer 答案依据为文章最后一句话。

测评：

题型 \ 正误题数	正确题数	错误题数
判断题		
选择题		
正确率		

备注：正确率达 80% 以上为优秀，70% 以上为良好，60% 以上为合格

▶**Passage two**

Reading Comprehension (Skimming and Scanning) (15 minutes)

Directions: *In this part, you will have 15 minutes to go over the passage quickly and answer the questions on Answer Sheet 1.*

For questions 1-7, mark

Y (*for YES*) *if the statement agrees with the information given in the passage;*

N (*for NO*) *if the statement contradicts the information given in the passage;*

NG (*for NOT GIVEN*) *if the information is not given in the passage.*

For questions 8-10, complete the sentences with the information given in the passage.

Computer Crime

A computer crime is generally defined as one that involves the use of computers and software for illegal purposes. This doesn't mean that all the crimes are new types of crime. On the contrary, many of these crimes, such as embezzlement of funds, the alteration of records, theft, vandalism, sabotage, and terrorism, can be committed without a computer. But with a computer, these offenses can be carried out more quickly and with less chance that the person responsible for the crime will be discovered.

Computer crimes are on the rise and have been for the last twelve years. Just how much these computer crimes cost the American public is in dispute, but estimates range from $3 billion to $5 billion annually. Even the FBI, which attempts to keep track of the growth or decline of all kinds of crimes, is unable to say precisely how large a loss is involved; however, it estimates that the average take from a company hit by computer crime is $600,000. A number of reasons are given for the increase in computer crime: (A) more computers in use and, thus, more people who are familiar with basic computer operation; (B) more computers tied together in satellite and other data — transmission networks; and (C) the easy access of microcomputers to huge mainframe data bases.

The Criminal

Movies and newspaper stories might lead us to believe that most computer crimes are committed by teenage "hackers" — brilliant and basically good children who let their imagination and technical genius get them into trouble. But a realistic look at the crimes reveals that the offender is likely to be an employee of the firm against which the crime has been committed, i. e. , an "insider".

Difficulty of Detection and Prevention

Given the kind of person who commits a computer crime and the environment in which the crime occurs, it is often difficult to detect who the criminal is. First of all, the crime may be so complex that months or years go by before anyone discovers it.

Second, once the crime has been revealed, it is not easy to find a clear trail of evidence that leads back to the guilty party. After all, looking for "weapons" or fingerprints does not occur as it might in the investigation of more conventional crimes.

Third, there are usually no witnesses to the computer crime, even though it may be taking place in a room filled with people. Who is to say if the person at the next terminal, calmly keying in data, is doing the company's work or committing a criminal act?

Fourth, not enough people in management and law enforcement know enough about computer technology to prevent the crimes. Authorities have to be familiar with the computer's capabilities within a given situation to guard against its misuses. In some large cities, such as Los Angeles, police departments have set up specially trained computer crime units.

But even when an offender is caught, the investigators, attorneys (律师), judges, or juries may find the alleged crime too complicated and perplexing to handle. More attorneys are specializing in computer law and studying the computer's potential for misuse.

After a computer crime has been discovered, many companies do not report it or prosecute (起诉) the person responsible. A company may not announce the crime out of fear that the pubic will find out the weaknesses of its computer system and lose confidence in its organization. Banks, credit card companies, and investment firms are especially sensitive about revealing their vulnerabilities (脆弱性) because they rely heavily on customer trust.

To avoid public attention, cautious companies will often settle cases of computer tampering out of court. And if cases do go to trial and the offenders are convicted, they may be punished only by a fine or light sentence because the judge or jury isn't fully trained to understand the nature and seriousness of the crime.

Not all companies are timid in apprehending computer criminals. For example, Connecticut General Life Insurance Company decided it had to get tough on violators. So when the company discovered that one of its computer technicians had embezzled $200,000 by entering false benefit claims, it presented it findings to the state's attorney and aided in the prosecution of the technician. The technician was found guilty and sentenced to prison, not just for the computer misuse, but also for grand theft and insurance fraud. Connecticut General now has a policy of reporting all incidents of theft or fraud, no matter how small.

提示：在实考试卷中，8～10 题在答题卡 1 上。

1. The FBI knows exactly how large a loss is involved in computer crimes.

2. It has become easy for microcomputer owners to use huge mainframe data bases.

3. It is implied in the Paragraph 3 that most computer criminals are the employees of the concerned companies.

4. Many companies don't report computer crimes because law procedures against computer crimes usually cost a lot of money.

5. When computer crime takes place in a room filled with people, there are usually many witnesses to the crime.

6. The passage is mainly about the increase of computer crimes in America and the difficulties in combating computer crimes.

7. Computer crimes are on the rise because more cheap microcomputers are available.

8. According to the passage, computer crimes has been on the rise for the last years.

9. Connecticut General Life Insurance company is cited as _____ of companies that took serious measures to fight against computer crimes.

10. Banks, credit card companies, and investment firms are especially sensitive about revealing their vulnerabilities because they place too much reliance on _____.

答案 1. N 2. Y 3. Y 4. N 5. N 6. Y 7. NG
8. twelve 9. an example 10. customer trust

解析：

1. N)。该句句意为：美国联邦调查局确切的知道计算机犯罪造成了多大损失。本题解题依据为本文第二段"Even the FBI, which

attempts… is involved"，该句大意为：尽管 FBI 对于各种犯罪的上升和下降有清晰认识，但并不能精确说明损失多大，所以与原文之意不合。

2. Y）。该句句意为：计算机拥有者很容易利用大量计算机数据库。本题解题依据为第二段最后一段话 "… the easy access of microcomputers to huge mainframe data bases." 与原文之意吻合。

3. Y）。该句句意为：本文第三段暗示大多数利用计算机犯罪者是相关公司雇员。本题解题依据为文章第三段最后一句话，其大意为：现实情况表明很可能是该公司雇员内部人……，与原文所述之意吻合。

4. N）。该句句意为：许多公司不举报计算机犯罪是因为法律诉讼通常花费很多钱。解题依据为本文第九段第一和第二句话，他们不举报是害怕公众发现其计算机系统的弱点而对其丧失信心。据此可确定与原文所述不符。

5. N）。该句句意为：当计算机犯罪在满是人的房间里发生时，通常有很多证人指证犯罪。本题解题依据为本文第六段第一句话，该句大意为：即使计算机犯罪发生在满是人的房间里，通常也无证人。据此可知该句所述之意与原文不符。

6. Y）。该句句意为：本篇文章主要是关于计算机犯罪的增长及与之作斗争的困难性，通览全文，尤其根据小标题的提示，我们不难看出文章主要论述了计算机犯罪与日俱增及难以发觉和阻止诸方面的原因，即文章的中心思想，与原文所述主旨吻合。

7. NG）。该句句意为：计算机犯罪上升是因为有更多便宜的计算机。本文第二段用 A，B，C 列出了计算机犯罪增加的三大原因，其中并未提及计算机便宜这一点。

8. twelve 答案依据为第二段第一句话。

9. an example "… be cited as an example"，表示"引用……来作为一个例证"答案依据为文章最后一段第二句话。但原文没有直接照抄的语言，只能根据理解完成此空。

10. customer trust 答案依据为本文第九段最后一句话。

测评:

题 型 \ 正误题数	正确题数	错误题数
判断题		
选择题		
正确率		

备注: 正确率达 80% 以上为优秀, 70% 以上为良好, 60% 以上为合格

▶Passage Three

Reading Comprehension (Skimming and Scanning) (15 minutes)

Directions: In this part, you will have 15 minutes to go over the passage quickly and answer the questions on Answer Sheet 1.

For questions 1-7, mark

Y (*for YES*)　　　　　*if the statement agrees with the information given in the passage;*

N (*for NO*)　　　　　*if the statement contradicts the information given in the passage;*

NG (*for NOT GIVEN*)　*if the information is not given in the passage.*

For questions 8-10, complete the sentences with the information given in the passage.

Spiders

Spiders can be distinguished from other Arachnids because the prosoma (combined head and thorax) is only separated from the opisthosoma (abdomen) by a narrow waist, in other Arachnids the whole body appears to be much more of a single unit. All spiders produce silk, but only some construct webs to catch their homes and to protect their eggs. All spiders possess poison glands but very few of them are dangerous to humans, of the 600 + species in Britain only 12 (at least one of these is a recent human assisted colonist) are strong enough to pierce the human skin, and apart from allergies, none are more dangerous than a common wasp. Most spiders have 8 eyes (though some have 6, 4, 2 or 0), as well as 8 legs. (by the way if you count the claws as separate leg section [which you shouldn't really] then their legs have 8 parts as well [coxa, trochanter, femur, patella, tibia, tarsus, metatarus, claws]) There are more than 32000 known species of spider in the world. No human being has ever been officially recorder as having died as the result of a 'tarantula' bite. All spiders are carnivorous and feed only on liquids, i. e. their preys natural juices and the breakdown products of external digestion (meaning they spit, exude or inject digestive juices onto/into their prey and suck up the resulting soup). So why not invite some to your next social do?

What's In a Name

The word 'Arachnida' comes from the Greek word 'Arachne' who was the daughter of Idmon of Colophon in Lydia, a dyer by trade. Arachne herself was a weaver, the best in all the known world. However in a foolish moment she challenged Athene, the daughter of Zeus and goddess of, among other things, waving to a weaving competition. Arachne wove so perfect a cloth that she tore it to shreds. Arachne became depressed after this and in the end she hung herself. Athene stirred to remorse at the knowledge of what her anger had wrought turned the rope Arachne had used to hang herself into a web and Arachne herself into a spider so that the beauty of her spinning should not be lost to the world ever again.

The Great Household Spider Safari

There are just over six hundred different sorts of spider in the British Isles. But of these only a handful are commonly found in houses. At the front of the head are a pair of what appear to be small legs. These are called palps and are used to guide food to the spider's mouth. The front of the head also has a group of six or eight eyes. On the underside of the body at the rear, are four or six small conical bumps or cylinders. There are the spinnerets from which the spider produces the silk to make its webs. Telling male and female spiders apart is easily done by looking at their palps. Males have swollen ends to their palps which makes them look as if they are wearing boxing gloves, these are often strange shapes if looked at with a hand lens. Females have normal looking palps that are not swollen at the ends. The largest spider is the Goliath spider, the female of which grows to reach a leg span of ten inches. The largest spider in Britain is the Cardinal spider which is a close cousin of Tim Tegenaria. Females can achieve a leg span of four and a half inches. It is known as the Cardinal spider as it was common in Hampton Court when Cardinal Wolsey lived there. The sight of these long legged spiders wandering around the palace at night used to frighten him. So far 32000 different kinds of spider have been discovered from all over the world. Britain has 630 different kinds of spider of which 250 are tiny Money spiders. The smallest of which has a body less than one millimeter long.

1. All the silk produced by spiders construct webs to catch their food.

2. Not all the poison glands possessed by spiders are dangerous to human beings.

3. Spiders often kill humans in Britain when they pierce human skin.

4. After seeing her enemy commits suicide, Arachne turned Athena into a spider.

5. Tim Tegenaria spiders are closely related to tarantula spiders; both are found in Britain.

6. So far 32000 different kinds of spiders have been discovered from all over the world.

7. Money spiders are the smallest spiders found in the Arachnids family.

8. There are more than _____ known species of spider in the world.

9. Telling male and female spiders apart is easily done by _____ .

10. The largest spider is _____ .

答案　1. N　2. Y　3. N　4. N　5. NG　6. Y　7. NG

　　　　8. 32000　9. looking at their pales　10. the Goliath spider

解析:

1. N)。当出现 all 这种过于绝对的词语时，考生应该引起注意。一般这样的命题多数是不正确的。首段中有句话："All spiders produce silk, but only some construct webs to catch their food" 命题中 all 的说法过于绝对。

2. Y)。该命题是对原文第二段首句话的同意改写。

3. N)。原文中第一段中写到，"of the 600 + spiders in Britain only 12 are strong enough to pierce the human skin"，因此并不是命题中说的当它们刺进人的皮肤会经常杀死人。

4. N)。原文中说，"Arachne became depressed after this and in the end she hung herself."注意代词 this 指代上面的句子，结合上一句一起理解，命题显然是错误的。

5. NG)。文章中只出现过一次 Tim Tegenaria，所以该题很好定位，即最后一段的第二句。可是文章中并没有出现 tarantula spiders。

6. Y)。该命题定位在最后一段倒数第三句话处。

7. NG)。首先定位 Money spiders 出现的位置是文章的最后的两句，可是并没有提到它是最小的。

8. 32000 该题由关键词 species of spider 定位在第一段倒数第二句。

9. looking at their pales 该题定位在倒数第二段的首句。

10. the Goliath spider 扫读全文的时候注意有最高级的地方。由此我们可以将该题定位在文章最后一段的首句。

测评:

题 型　　正误题数	正确题数	错误题数
判断题		
选择题		
正确率		

备注: 正确率达80%以上为优秀, 70%以上为良好, 60%以上为合格

▶**Passage Four**

Reading Comprehension (Skimming and Scanning) (15 minutes)

Directions: *In this part, you will have 15 minutes to go over the passage quickly and answer the questions on Answer Sheet 1.*

For questions 1-7, mark

Y (for YES)　　　　　　*if the statement agrees with the information given in the passage;*

N (for NO)　　　　　　*if the statement contradicts the information given in the passage;*

NG (for NOT GIVEN)　*if the information is not given in the passage.*

For questions 8-10, complete the sentences with the information given in the passage.

OGAMA, Japan, this mountain village on the West Coast, withered (枯萎) to eight aging residents, concluded recently that it could no longer go on. So, after months of anguish, the villagers settled on a drastic solution; selling all of Ogama to an industrial waste company from Tokyo, which will trun it into a landfill.

With the proceeds, the villagers plan to pack up everything, including their family graves, and move in the next few years to yet uncertain destinations, most likely becoming the first community in Japan to cease to exist voluntarily.

"I'm sure we're the first ones to have made such a proposal,", said Kazuo Miyasaka, 64, thevillage leader. "It's because there's no future for us here, zero."

On a hill overlooking a field of overgrown bushes, surrounded by the sounds of a running stream and a bush warbler (鸣鸟), Miyasaka pointed below with his right index finger. "I never imagined it would come to this," he said. "I mean, those all used to be rice fields."

Ogama's decision, though extreme, points to a larger problem beetting Japan, which has one of the world's fastest-graying societies and whose population began declinlng last year for the first time. As rural Japan becomes increasingly depopulated, many villages and hamlets (小村) like Ogama, along with their traditions and histories, risk vanishing.

Japan is dotted with so many such communities that academics have coined a term — "villages that have reached their limits" — to describe those with populations that are more than half elderly. Out of 140 villages in Monzen, the municipality that includes Ogama, 40 percent have fewer than 10 households, inhabited mostly by ghe elderly.

Rural Japan has never recovered from its long recession, unlike urban areas. Many of its commercial main streets have been reduced to what the Japanese call "shuttered streets," and few rural areas have found economic alternatives to the huge public works projects that the long-governing Liberal Democratic Party kept doling out.

During his five years in office, Prime Minister Junichiro Koizumi has reduced public works spending that yielded money and jobs to local construction companies.

Koizumi cut subsidies and tax redistribution to local governments, instead giving them the power to collect taxes directly But rural officials argue that with a decreasing population and few businesses, there are few taxes to collect.

In keeping with a nationwide movement to combine financially squeezed municipalities, Monzen merged with nearby Wajima City in February. In 2000, revenue from the national government to the two municipalities totaled $114 million, accounting for 50 percent of their overall revenue; in 2005, money from the capital fell to $90 million, or 44 percent of revenue.

Fumiaki Kaji, mayor of the merged municipality, said recent changes amounted to a "simple logic of telling the countryside that it should die."

Ogama lies in a valley in a mountain facing the sea, reached by a single-lane road that winds its way through a deep green forest where foxes and raccoon dogs are spotted regularly. The road ends here.

Bunzo Mizushiri, 81, a historian in Wajima, said Ogama (whose name means "Big Pot") was the place where monks cleansed themselves before going up Takatusme, a sacred mountain.

After World War Ⅱ, there were about 30 households here, each with eight or nine people. Today, three couples live in one corner of the village, and two women live alone in another corner. A small hill rises in the center, atop which stands a Shinto (日本的神道教) shrine whose gate was partly felled by an earthquake years ago.

Small streams flow from the surrounding mountains, keeping the ground here moist and covered with patches of moss. The expanding forest has begun reclaiming once cultivated land, hiding the ruins of abandoned housed, and blocking the sunlight.

"Our house is still standing, thankfully," said Harue Miyasaka, the village leader's wife and, at 61, Ogama's youngest inhabitant. "But when you look at the houses collapsing one after another, you understand what's ahead for your own house."

"We're at a dead-end here," she said in front of her house, where the single-lane road reached its end. "Our children haven't come back, so there's no further growth. We'll just keep getting older."

Her husband first proposed the idea. After retiring as a seaman two decades ago and setting up a roof-waterproofing business, Kazuo Miyasaka said he foresaw Ogama's shrinking future. So about 15 years ago, he began pursuing several possibilities, including turning the area into a golf course. None of the ideas went anywhere until he approached Takeei, a Tokyo industrial waste company, a couple of years ago. Takeei was interested.

Miyasaka summoned the entire village — he became its permanent chief three years ago after Ogama's two other men could no longer take turns as leader because of poor health — and told his neighbors about the offer.

"If young people came back, these villages could go on," Kenichi Taniguchi, 76, said. "But that's not happening. They're all dying out."

1. No community in Japan choose to stop existence in their living place before Ogama.

2. With the decrease of rural population in Japan, many villages and their cultures are likely to disappear.

3. Both the rural areas and urban areas in Japan haven't recovered from the long recession.

4. Rural officials say they can collect few taxes because of the backward economic development.

5. Many municipalities combined to solve the financial problem and it worked.

6. According to Bunzo Mizushiri, there is no monk who cleanses himself before climbing Takatsume now.

7. The forest expands to the area where used to be cultivated land and the ruins of abandoned houses in Ogama.

8. Harue Miyasaka Knew that her house would also _____.

9. Miyasaka proposed to build _____ in Ogama, which attracted Takeei's interst.

10. Only if _____, can the villages that have reached their limits survive, according to Kenichi Taniguchi.

答案 1. Y 2. Y 3. N 4. N 5. N 6. NG 7. Y
8. collapse 9. a landfill 10. young people come back

解析：

1. Y)。题干中的 choose to stop existence 与原文 cease to exist voluntarily 属于同意表达。题干表述正确。

2. Y)。原文 depopulated, rising vanishing 与题目 decrease, gradually disappear 属于同意表达，题干是原文的同意转述。

3. N)。原文说日本农村一直没有从大萧条中复苏，这与城市不同。可知城市摆脱了萧条。题干与原文不符。

4. N)。原文说农村地区的官员分析的税收微薄的原因：由于农村人口的不断减少，再加上没有多少企业。题干所说的原因"经济发展落后"与原文不符，选 N。

5. N)。本段提到了许多政府由于财力拮据，开始合并。但合并后，政府拨付的财税收入同时也在减少。所以题干说合并"起作用了"是不对的。

6. NG)。原文讲述的是 81 岁历史学家 Bunzo Mizushiri 介绍的大釜村历史。但是原文没有提现在的情况。

7. Y)。原文说日益扩张的森林开始吞噬原先开垦过的土地，覆盖了被遗弃的房屋，遮住了阳光，题干是原文的同意转述。

8. 本段宫坂春惠对自己房子未来的猜想："周围的房子都在倒塌，你就知道你自己的房子将来会怎么样了"所以答案是 collapse。

9. 原文提到 Miyasaka 提出很多建议。最后只有 Takeei，一家工业废品处理公司感兴趣。也就是第一段中提到的那家公司。所以宫坂的建议应该是垃圾填埋场，答案是 a landfill。

10. 题干中的 survive 与原文 could go on 属于转述表达。注意句中的虚拟语气，答案是 young people come back。

测评：

题　型	正误题数	正确题数	错误题数
判断题			
选择题			
正确率			

备注：正确率达 80% 以上为优秀，70% 以上为良好，60% 以上为合格

▶Passag Five

Reading Comprehension（Skimming and Scanning）（15 minutes）

Directions: In this part, you will have 15 minutes to go over the passage quickly and answer the questions on Answer Sheet 1.

For questions 1-7, choose the best answer frem the four choices marked A）、B）、C）、D）.

For questions 8-10, complete the sentences with the information given in the passage.

That's enough, kids.

It was a lovely day at the park and Stella Bianchi was enjoying the sunshine with her two children when a young boy, aged about four, approached her two-year-old son and pushed him to the ground.

"I'd watched him for a little while and my son was the fourth or fifth child he'd shoved," she says. "I went over to them, picked up my son, turned to the boy and said, firmly, 'No, we don't push,'" What happened next was unexpected.

"The boy's mother ran toward me from across the park," Stella says, "I thought she was coming over to apologize, but instead she started shouting at me for disciplining her child, All I did was let him know his behavior was unacceptable. Was I supposed to sit back while her kid did whatever he wanted, hurting other children in the process?"

Getting your own children to play nice is difficult enough. Dealing with other people's children has become a minefield.

In my house, jumping on the sofa is not allowed. In my sister's house it's encouraged. For her, it's about kids being kids: " If you can't do it at three, when can you do it?"

Each of these philosophies is valid and, it has to be said, my son loves visiting his aunt's house. But I find myself saying "no" a lot when her kids are over at mine. That's OK between sisters but becomes dangerous territory when you're talking to the children of friends or acquaintances.

"Kids aren't all raised the same," agrees Professor Naomi White of Monash University. " But there is still an idea that they're the property of the parent. We see our children as an extension of ourselves, so if you're saying that my child is behaving inappropriately, then that's somehow a criticism of me."

In those circumstances, it's difficult to know whether to approach the child directly or the parent first. There are two schools of thought.

"I'd go to the child first," says Andrew Fuller, author of Tricky Kids. Usually a quiet reminder that 'we don't do that here' is enough. Kids nave finely tuned antennae (直觉) for how to behave in different settings."

He points out bringing it up with the parent first may make them feel neglectful, which could cause problems. Of course, approaching the child first can bring its own headaches, too.

This is why White recommends that you approach the parents first. Raise your concerns with the parents if they're there and ask them to deal with it," she says.

Asked how to approach a parent in this situation, psychologist Meredith Fuller answers: " Explain your needs as well as stressing the importance of the friendship. Preface your remarks with something like: 'I know you'll think I'm silly but in my house I don't want..."

When it comes to situations where you're caring for another child, white is straightforward: "common sense must prevail. If things don't go well, then have a chat."

There're a couple of new grey areas. Physical punishment, once accepted from any adult, is no longer appropriate. "A new set of considerations has come to the fore as part of the debate about how we handle children."

For Andrew Fuller, the child-centric nature of our society has affected everyone: " The rules are different now from when today's parents were growing up," he says, "Adults are scared of saying: ' don't swear', or asking a child to stand up on a bus. They're worried that there will be conflict if they point these things out — either from older children, or their parents."

He sees it as a loss of the sense of common public good and public courtesy (礼貌), and says that adults suffer form it as much as child.

Meredith Fuller agrees: "A code of conduct is hard to create when you're living in a world in which everyone is exhausted from overwork and lack of sleep, and a world in which nice people are perceived to finish last."

"it's about what I'm doing and what I need," Andrew Fuller says. "the days when a kid came home from school and said, " I got into trouble ". And dad said, ' you probably deserved it'. Are over. Now the parents are charging up to the school to have a go at teachers."

This jumping to our children's defense is part of what fuels the "walking on eggshells" feeling that surrounds our dealings with other people's children. You know that if you remonstrate (劝诫) with the child, you're going to have to deal with the parent. it's admirable to be protective of our kids, but is it good?

"Children have to learn to negotiate the world on their own, within reasonable boundaries," White says. "I suspect that it's only certain sectors of the population doing the running to the school — better —

educated parents are probably more likely to be too involved. "

White believes our notions of a more child-centred, it's a way of talking about treating our children like commodities (商品). We're centred on them but in ways that reflect positively on us. We treat them as objects whose appearance and achievements are something we can be proud of, rather than serve the best interests of the children. "

One way over-worked, under-resourced parents show commitment to their children is to leap to their defense. Back at the park, Bianchi's intervention (干预) on her son's behalf ended in an undignified exchange of insulting words with the other boy's mother.

As Bianchi approached the park bench where she'd been sitting, other mums came up to her and congratulated her on taking a stand. "Apparently the boy had a longstanding reputation for bad behavior and his mum for even worse behavior if he was challenged. "

Andrew Fuller doesn't believe that we should be afraid of dealing with other people's kids. "look at kids that aren't your own as a potential minefield," he says. He recommends that we don't stay silent over inappropriate behavior, particularly with regular visitors.

1. What did Stella Bianchi expect the young boy's mother to do when she talked to him?

    A) Make an apology.

    B) Come over to intervene.

    C) Discipline her own boy.

    D) Take her own boy away.

2. What does the author say about dealing with other people's children?

    A) It's important not to hurt them in any way.

    B) It's no use trying to stop their wrongdoing.

    C) It's advisable to treat them as one's own kids.

    D) It's possible for one to get into lot of troubles.

3. According to professor Naomi white of Monash university, when one's

kids are criticized, their parents will probably feel _____.

A) discouraged

B) hurt

C) puzzled

D) overwhelmed

4. What should one do when seeing other people's kids misbehave according to Andrew fuller?

A) Talk to them directly in a mild way.

B) Complain to their parents politely.

C) Simply leave them alone.

D) Punish them lightly.

5. Due to the child-centric nature of our society, _____.

A) parents are worried when their kids swear at them

B) people think it improper to criticize kids in public

C) people are reluctant to point our kids' wrongdoings

D) many conflicts arise between parents and their kids

6. In a world where everyone is exhausted from over work and lack of sleep, _____.

A) it's easy for people to become impatient

B) it's difficult to create a code of conduct

C) it's important to be friendly to everybody

D) it's hard for people to admire each other

7. How did people use to respond when their kids got into trouble at school?

A) They'd question the teachers.

B) They'd charge up to the school.

C) They'd tell the kids to clam down.

D) They'd put the blame on their kids.

8. Professor white believes that the notions of a more child-centred society should be _____.

9. According to professor white, today's parents treat their children as

something they _____.

10. Andrew fuller suggests that , when kids behave inappropriately, people should not _____.

答案 1. A 2. D 3. B 4. A 5. C 6. B 7. D

8. challenged

9. can be proud of

10. stay silent

第二节　篇章词汇阅读与简答测与评

▶**Passage one**

Directions: In this section, there is a passage with ten blanks. You are required to select one word for each blank from a list of choices given in a word bank following the passage. Read the passage through carefully before making your choices. Each choice in the bank is identified by a letter. Please mark the corresponding letter for each item on Answer Sheet 2 with a single line through the centre. You may not use any of the words in the bank more than once.

El Nino is the name given to the mysterious and often unpredictable change in the climate of the world. This strange ___1___ happens every five to eight years. It starts in the Pacific Ocean and is thought to be caused by a failure in the trade winds, which affects the ocean currents driven by these winds. As the trade winds lessen in ___2___, the ocean temperatures rise, causing the Peru current flowing in from the east to warm up by as much as 5°C.

The warming of the ocean has far-reaching effects. The hot, humid air over the ocean causes severe ___3___ thunderstorms. The rainfall is increased across South America ___4___ floods to Peru. In the West Pacific, there are droughts affecting Australia and Indonesia. So while some parts or the world prepare for heavy rains and floods, other parts face drought, poor crops and ___5___.

El Nino usually lasts for about 18 months. The 1982-83 El Nino brought the most ___6___ weather in modern history. Its effect was worldwide and it left more than 2,000 people dead and caused over eight billon pounds ___7___ of damage. The 1990 El Nino lasted until June 1995. Scientists ___8___ this to be the longest El Nino for 2,000 years.

Nowadays, weather expert are able to forecast when an El Nino will ___9___, buy they still not ___10___ sure what leads to it or what affects how strong it will be.

A) estimate   B) strength   C) deliberately   D) notify
E) tropical   F) phenomenon   G) stable   H) attraction
I) completely   J) destructive   K) starvation   L) bringing
M) exhaustion   N) worth   O) strike

答案　1. F　2. B　3. E　4. L　5. K
　　　　6. J　7. N　8. A　9. O　10. I

解析:

1. F)。文章的开头主要介绍了"厄尔尼诺"的由来；本题应该填入一个名词作为"happens"的主语，而前面的 this 就是指代"厄尔尼诺"，所以答案为表示现象的名词 F。含义是"这种奇怪的现象每 5~8 年就会发生"。

2. B)。此题要填的词是位于介词之后，我们就可以想到介宾短语的搭配，也就是选择名词；从选项中我们可以看到"strength"是正确答案；意为"随着季风力量的减弱……"。

3. E)。从整句话的翻译可以看出"海洋上的闷热潮湿的空气能够引起……风暴"，很明显的看出，空白处应该填一个形容词来修饰这个名词"风暴"，而只有 E（热带的）最符合文章的内容。

4. L)。从整个句子我们能够看出，空白处的前面是一个主语、谓语和状语的结构，而空白处的后面带定语的名词；通过前面的主谓状结构可以看出后面的 floods 只能是名词而不是动词，所以空白处只能为非谓语动词和介词，根据文章的上下文，只有 L 是答案"整个南非降雨量增大，并把洪水都引向秘鲁"。

5. K)。空白处提到了"厄尔尼诺"现象所带来坏的影响，而且这个句子出现了一连串的名词，故答案选择 K)。此句的含义为"因此，当世界的某些部分遭遇倾盆大雨、洪涝灾害的时候，世界上有些地方却可能遭遇干旱、收成不好或者饥荒"。

6. J)。"1982～1983 年的厄尔尼诺现象引起了当今世界最具有——气候状况"，我们可以得知空白处填的是形容词，根据文章含义，只有选项 J 合适。

7. N)。题干中的空白处后面是一个 of 的短语，而它之前又是一连串的数字又说明此空所填的要与数字有关，只有 N 最合适。意思是"它造成世界范围内的破坏，引起 2000 多人丧生，造成 80 多亿英镑的经济损失"。

8. A)。本题考查的是固定搭配，应该是"... to 再接表示名词的词"，空白处应该是一个动词，只有 A 符合选项。

9. O)。"现在，气象的专家们能够预测厄尔尼诺现象在什么时候会——"根据上下文以及剩下的选项得知 O 是正确的选项。

10. I)。"但是他们也不是——确定到底是什么原因引起这种现象的发生"，我们可以判断修饰 sure 的词一定是一个副词，所以为 completely，答案 I 是正确的。

测评：

题型 \ 正误题数	正确题数	错误题数
选择题		
正确率		
备注：正确率达 80% 以上为优秀，70% 以上为良好，60% 以上为合格		

▶**Passage two**

Directions: In this section, there is a passage with ten blanks. You are required to select one word for each blank from a list of choices given in a word bank following the passage. Read the passage through carefully before making your choices. Each choice in the bank is identified by a letter. Please mark the corresponding letter for each item on Answer Sheet 2 with a single line through the centre. You may not use any of the words in the bank more than once.

The flood of women into the job market boosted economic growth and changed U. S. society in many ways. Many in-home jobs that used to be done __1__ by women — ranging from family shopping to preparing meals to doing __2__ work-still need to be done by someone. Husbands and children now do some of these jobs, a __3__ that has changed the target market for many products. Or a working woman may face a crushing "poverty of time" and look for help elsewhere, creating opportunities for producers of frozen meals, child care centers, dry cleaners, financial services, and the like.

Although there is still a big wage __4__ between men and women, the income working women __5__ gives them new independence and buying power. For example, women now __6__ about half of all cars. Not long ago, many cars dealers __7__ women shoppers by ignoring them or suggesting that they come back with their husbands. Now car companies have realized that women are __8__ customers. It's interesting that some leading Japanese car dealers were the first to __9__ pay attention to women customers. In Japan, fewer women have jobs or buy cars — the Japanese society is still very much male-oriented. Perhaps it was the __10__ contrast with Japanese society that prompted American firms to pay more attention to women buyers.

A) scale   B) retailed   C) generate   D) extreme
E) technically   F) affordable   G) situation   H) really
I) potential   J) gap   K) voluntary   L) excessive
M) insulted   N) purchase   O) primarily

解析:

1. O)。从空白处前后的句子可以看出此处应该为一个副词来使整个句子能够衔接起来。选项中 technically, primarily, really 中只有 primarily 符合文章的含义"很多在家办公的工作主要都是由女性来完成的"。

2. K)。空白处前面是 doing,后面是 work,可以明显的判断出此处应该为一个形容词修饰这个 work。句子的含义是"从家庭购物到准备事物来做一些志愿的工作"。

3. G)。空白处前面是个冠词 a。可以判断出此处为一个名词,名词中包括 situation,scale 和 gap。从 that 后面句子可以分析出此处的名词是要介绍的一个情况。

4. J)。句子的含义是"尽管女性和男性之间有一个很大的工资——"根据文章前段的分析,再根据一些常识,可以判断出空格处的名词的含义应该是 gap(代沟)。

5. C)。句子的含义是"女性工作赚的工资给予了她们新的独立"句子的主语是 income,谓语是 gives。此处为动词应该修饰 working women。选项中 C 的含义是 generate(产生、发生)。

6. N)。根据句子的含义很容易分析出空白处缺少的是谓语部分。而句子中的 now 为现在时态。很容易判断出答案为 N(购买)。

7. M)。空白处在句子中充当是谓语成分,从空白处后面的句子可以看出汽车销售员都是忽视女性并且很歧视她们。选项(insulted)符合句子的含义。

8. I)。空白处后面的句子为名词,可以判断出此处应该为形容词。而 customer 是客户的意思。女性现在变得有钱了,而此处也把女性暗示为"潜在的客户"。

9. H)。句子的含义是"很有趣的是,一些主导日本汽车的销售人员是第一次关注女性消费者"。可以判断出空白处的词性是副词,在 really 和 technically 中,只有 really 正确。

10. D)。空白处的词性应该为形容词,来修饰后面的 contrast,而 contrast 是对比,比较的含义。根据句子的含义"日本是男性主

导的国家，不过也是第一个真正关注女性消费的国家"。前后是
两种极端的对比。

测评：

题 型　　正误题数	正确题数	错误题数
选择题		
正确率		

备注：正确率达80%以上为优秀，70%以上为良好，60%以上为合格

▶Passage three

Directions: In this section, there is a passage with ten blanks. You are required to select one word for each blank from a list of choices given in a word bank following the passage. Read the passage through carefully before making your choices. Each choice in the bank is identified by a letter. Please mark the corresponding letter for each item on Answer Sheet 2 with a single line through the centre. You may not use any of the words in the bank more than once.

As is known to all, the organization and management of wages and salaries are very complex.

Generally speaking, the Accounts Department is ___1___ for calculations of pay, while the Personnel Department is interested in discussions with the employees about pay.

If a firm wants to ___2___ a new wage and salary structure, it is essential that the firm should decide on a ___3___ of job evaluation and ways of measuring the performance of its employees. In order to be ___4___, that new pay structure will need agreement between Trade Unions and employers. In job evaluation, all of the requirements of each job are defined in a detailed job description. Each of those requirements is given a value, usually in "points", which are ___5___ together to give a total value for the job. For middle and higher management, a special method is used to evaluate managers on their knowledge of the job, their responsibility, and their ___6___ to solve problems. Because of the difficulty in measuring management work, however, job grades for managers are often decided without ___7___ to an evaluation system based on points.

In attempting to design a pay system, the Personnel Department should ___8___ the value of each job with these in the job market. ___9___, payment for a job should vary with any differences in the way that the job is performed. Where it is simple to measure the work done, as in the works done with hands, monetary encouragement schemes are often chosen, for ___10___ workers, where measurement is difficult, methods of additional payments are employed.

A) compare   B) responsible   C) useful   D) added
E) find   F) reference   G) indirect H) method
I) successful J) combined   K) Necessarily L) capacity
M) ability   N) Basically   O) adopt

答案 1. B 2. O 3. H 4. I 5. D
6. M 7. F 8. A 9. K 10. G

解析:

1. 选 B)。此处应填形容词。原文意思为"会计部门……计算报酬",选项中的形容词 responsible "负责任的", useful "有用的", indirect "间接的", successful "成功的", 其中 indirect 不能与 for 连用, 排除; 剩余几项中只有 B) responsible 意义符合原句, 其他均不符合, 故排除。

2. 选 O)。此处应填动词原形。本文主题就是采用一种新的工资和薪水制度时需要注意的问题, 选项中的动词原形有 compare "比较", find "找到", adopt "采纳", 分别带入原文, 只有 adopt 最符合原文意思, 故选 O) adopt。

3. 选 H）。此处应填名词。从原文看，and 连接并列结构，所以要填的词应与 and 后面的 ways 意思一致，选项中的名词只有 mathod = ways，故选 H）method。

4. 选 I）。此处应填形容词。上文说新的工资制度需要一套决定工作评估和衡量雇员表现的方法，说的是制度"是否有用"的问题。这句说的是新的工资制度执行过程中的问题，劳资双方先期达成一致是薪酬制度成功的必要条件。形容词 useful 和 successful，seccessful 更符合原文意思。

5. 选 D）。此处应填动词。这个动词的宾语是 point "分值"，把分值……起来 to give a total value "得出总分值"，选项中有 added 和 combined，前者指"把……相加"，后者意为"把……结合在一起"，原文指将分值相加得出总分，故 D）added 最符合文意。

6. 选 M）。此处应填名词。首先 solve problem "解决问题"是经理们应具备的能力，选项中的 capacity 与 ability 都可以表示"能力"；前者强调的是理解的能力和接受事物的能力，而后者强调实际应用的能力，故不难判断解决问题的能力应该用 M）ability。

7. 选 F）此处应填名词。前半句指出"因为管理工作很难评估，经理的工作得分不需要参照基于分值的评估系统决定。"without reference to 为固定搭配，意思是"与……无关"。故选 F）reference。

8. 选 A）。此处应填动词原形。原句中出现了 the value of each job "每种工作的价值"和 these in the job market "工作市场上的（工作价值）"，说明人事部门通过比较两种价值来计算工资制度。选项中只有 compare 表示"比较"，所以 A）compare 正确。

9. 选 K）。此处应填副词，修饰整句话。"报酬要随工作表现各方面的不同而有所改变"，选项中 Necessarily "必须地"与 Basically "基本地"为副词，分别带入原文，"报酬……的变化是必须的"更符合上下文意思，故排除 N），选 K）Necessarily。

10. 选 G）。此处应填形容词。前文中提到一种情况即 simple to measure the work done "易于评估的工作"，通常用现金奖励办法；而……measurement is difficult "难于评估的"，说明这些工作人员的工作不像手工工作那么直接，因而是间接的，故选项中只有 G) indirect 符合原句的意思。

测评：

题 型 ＼ 正误题数	正确题数	错误题数
选择题		
正确率		

备注：正确率达 80％ 以上为优秀，70％ 以上为良好，60％ 以上为合格

▶**Passage four**

Directions: *In this section, there is a passage with ten blanks. You are required to select one word for each blank from a list of choices given in a word bank following the passage. Read the passage through carefully before making your choices. Each choice in the bank is identified by a letter. Please mark the corresponding letter for each item on Answer Sheet 2 with a single line through the centre. You may not use any of the words in the bank more than once.*

Britain is not just one country and one people; even if some of its inhabitants think so. Britain is, in fact, a nation which can be divided into several __1__ parts, each part being an individual country with its own language, character and cultural __2__. Thus Scotland, Northern Ireland and Wales do not claim to __3__ to "England" because their inhabitants are not __4__ "English". They are Scottish, Irish or Welsh and many of them prefer to speak their own native tongue, which in turn is __5__ to the others.

These cultural minorities（少数民族）have been Britain's original inhabitants. In varying degrees they have managed to __6__ their national characteristics, and their particular customs and way of life. This is probably even more ture of the __7__ areas where traditional ife has not

been so affected by the __8__ of industrialism as the border areas have
been. The Celtic races are said to be more emotional by nature than the
English. An Irish temper is legendary. The Scots could rather __9__
about their reputation for excessive thrift and prefer to be remembered for
their folk songs and dances, while the Welsh are famous for their singing.
The Celtic __10__ as a whole produces humorous writers and artists, such
as the Irish Bernard Shaw, the Scottish Robert Burns, and the Welsh
Dylan Thomas, to mention but a few.

A) incomprehensible B) temper   C) remote   D) separate
E) understandable   F) forget   G) generally   H) temperament
I) preserve   J) strictly   K) traditional L) reserve
M) growth   N) apply   O) belong

答案 1. D 2. K 3. O 4. J 5. A
6. I 7. C 8. M 9. F 10. H

解析：

1. 选 D)。此处应填形容词，修饰名词 parts。文章首句即提出观点
   Britain is not just one country and one people "英国不只是一个国家
   和一个民族"，又从后文的 invided into, each part 以及 Individual
   country 可知英国被分成几个分离的部分，选项中只有 separate 表
   达了这个意思，故 D) separate 正确。

2. 选 K)。此处应填名词。选项中有四个单词 temper, temperament,
   traditions 和 growth，语言等是一个民族的文化传统，故这里应该
   填 K) traditions，其他几个名词不符合上下文。

3. 选 O)。此处应填动词原形。前文中说明英国被分成独立的几部
   分，各自保存自己的文化传统；后文中 because……说明苏格兰、
   北爱尔兰以及威尔士的居民不承认自己是 "English"，说明他们
   并不承认自己属于 "England"，故这里应该选择 O) belong。
   apply 也可以和 to 连用，但 apply to 表示 "将……应用于"，不符
   合上下文意思。

4. 选 J）。此处应填形容词或副词。选项中的副词有 generally 和 strictly，文中要表达的意思是因为这几个部分都有自己的语言和文化传统，所以严格来说，他们不是"English"，但他们都属于 England。故 J）strictly 符合文意。generally "一般地，大体地"放在原文意义上不够严谨。三个形容词不能使语意通顺。

5. 选 A）。从前文中 prefer to speak their own native tongue 即苏格兰语、苏格兰语和威尔士语，那么就不难从选项中的 incomprehensible 和 understandable 中选择前者，故 A）incomprehensible "不能理解的"正确。

6. 选 I）。由 manage to 结构可知此处要填的是动词原形。选项中的动词原形还有 forget，preserve 和 reserve。从下文中 traditional life has not been so affected，可知他们成功地保存了自己的传统，排除 forget；reserve 和 presserve 都有"保存"的意思，前者指存留起来以派别的用场，后者指想办法保持原样，强调抵制破坏因素，故 I）preserve 符合文意。

7. 选 C）。此处应填形容词。从后文 where traditional life has not been so affected by the... of industrialis "人们的传统生活受工业化……的影响没有那么大的地方"可以推知，这些地方是比较偏远的地方，选项中的 C）remote "偏僻的，遥远的"符合上下文意思。

8. 选 M）。border area "边界地区"的工业化发展比 remote area 要快，所以此处要填的词是表示上升、增长的词，表示工业化的发展，选项 M）growth "增长，发展"符合上下文意思。

9. 选 F）。would rather 和 prefer 意思相同，后面是宁愿让人记住他们好的东西：民歌，舞蹈等。前面说的是过分节俭的坏名声，所以填入动词的意思应该与 remember 意思相反，选项中的 F）forget 符合上下文意思。

10. 选 H）。此处应填名词。选项中的名词还有 temper 和 temperament。前者指脾气，指情绪上的主要特征，后者指特征、气质，尤指带感情色彩的个性和在社交上的个性。这里指的是整个凯尔特民族的特征，故 H）temperament 正确。

测评：

题　型 　　正误题数	正确题数	错误题数
选择题		
正确率		

备注：正确率达80％以上为优秀，70％以上为良好，60％以上为合格

▶Passage five

Directions: In this section, there is a passage with ten blanks. You are required to select one word for each blank from a list of choices given in a word bank following the passage. Read the passage through carefully before making your choices. Each choice in the bank is identified by a letter. Please mark the corresponding letter for each item on Answer Sheet 2 with a single line through the centre. You may not use any of the words in the bank more than once.

Americans are proud of their variety and individualty, yet they love and respect few things more than a uniform. Why are uniforms so ___1___ in the United States?

Among the arguments for uniforms, one of the first is that in the eyes of most people they look more ___2___ than civilian （百姓的） clothes. People have become conditioned to ___3___ superior quality from a man who wears a uniform. The television repairman who wears a uniform tends to ___4___ more trust than one who appears in civilian clothes. Faith in the ___5___ of a garage mechanic is increased by a uniform. What an easier way is there for a nurse, a policeman, a barber, or a waiter to ___6___ professional identity （身份） than to step out of uniform? Uniforms also have many ___7___ benefits. They save on other clothes.

They save on laundry bills. They are often more comfortable and more durable than civilian clothes.

Primary among the arguments against uniforms is their lack of variety and the consequent loss of ___8___ experienced by people who must wear them. Though there are many types of uniforms, the wearer of any particular type is generally stuck with it, without ___9___, until retirement. When people look alike, they tend to think, speak, and act ___10___, on the job at least.

A) skill   B) popular   C) get   D) change
E) similarly   F) professional G) character   H) individuality
I) inspire   J) differently   K) expect   L) practical
M) recall   N) lose   O) ordinary

答案 1. B 2. F 3. K 4. I 5. A
6. N 7. L 8. H 9. D 10. E

解析:

1. 选 B)。从文章的第一句 they love and respect few things more than a uniform "他们又无比热爱和崇尚制服",说明了制服在美国很受欢迎。因此选项 B) popular 符合原文意思。选项中的 professional "职业的"、practical "实用的" 和 ordinary "普通的,平常的" 都不符合第一段的意思。

2. 选 F)。此处应填形容词。从 more... than civilian clothes 可知,此处要填的形容词意思与 civilian 相对,说明制服的特点。选项中的形容词中只有 professional "职业的" 和 civilian 相对的,故 F) professional 正确。而 pratical "实用的" 和 ordinary "平常的" 意思都不能和 civilian 对应,故排除。

3. 选 K)。由 be conditioned to do sth. "习惯于" 可知,此处应填动词原形。从前面的 look more "看起来更……" 和后面的 tend to "倾向于" 可知,这段要说明的是人们的主观印象,应填入表示 "期望(得到)" 的单词,只有 K) expect 符合原文语气。选项中 get "得到" 与上下文的语气不符合。

4. 选 I)。此处应填动词原形。从原文中"人们习惯……从穿制服的人那儿得到优质服务。"可知，人们更信任穿制服的人，即制服能使人产生信任感。选项中的动词原形中只有 I) inspire "使产生"符合文章。

5. 选 A)。此处应填名词。前面两句表达了人们对穿制服的人更加信任的意思，那么对于 garage mechanic "汽车修理工"来说，人们信任的是它的技术，而不是人品，故选项中只有 A) skill 符合原文意思。

6. 选 N)。此处应填动词。… step out of uniform "脱掉制服"是对护士、警察等职业来说是……职业身份的很简单的方式。脱下制服就失去了职业身份，由此可以推知此处填 N) lose。

7. 选 L)。此处应填形容词，说明制服的其他优点。从下文"……节省购买其他衣服的开销，节省洗衣费用，比便服更舒适也更耐穿"可知，制服除了增加信任感还有实际的优点。选项中 pratical "实用的"和 ordinary "平常的"，很明显 L) pratical 符合原文意思。

8. 选 H)。此处应填名词。文章首段就说"美国人为自己的多元化和个性化感到骄傲无比，然而他们又无比热爱和崇尚制服"，其中包含制服使他们失去自己个性的意思，那么联系第一段，此处指出的制服的缺点即为失去个性，故选项 H) individuality 正确。individuality 强调与他人特点的区别，而 character 指的是个人特定的内在本质。

9. 选 D)。此处应填名词。前面说制服让人失去了个性，虽然有很多种制服，但穿上制服的人直至退休都是那件制服，所以是没有变化的，故此处应填 change，故 D) change 正确。

10. 选 E)。此处应填副词，修饰动词 act。前面指出 … look alike, they tend to…，说明此处填的词和 alike 意思相近。选项中副词有 similarly 和 differently，很明显，E) similarly 与 alike 意思相近，故选 E) similarly。

测评:

题 型	正误题数	正确题数	错误题数
选择题			
正确率			

备注:正确率达80%以上为优秀,70%以上为良好,60%以上为合格

第三节　篇章阅读理解测与评

▶**Passage one**

Directions: Each passage is followed by some questions or unfinished statements. For each of them there are four choices marked A), B), C) and D). You should decide on the best choice.

If you want to teach your children how to say sorry, you must be good at saying it yourself, especially to your own children. But how you say it can be quite tricky.

If you say to your children "I'm sorry I got angry with you, but..." what follows that "but" can render the apology ineffective: "I had a bad day" or "your noise was giving me a headache" leaves the person who has been injured feeling that he should be apologizing for his bad behavior in expecting an apology.

Another method by which people appear to apologize without actually doing so is to say "I'm sorry you're upset"; this suggests that you are somehow at fault for allowing yourself to get upset by what the other person has done.

Then there is the general, all covering apology, which avoids the necessity of identifying a specific act that was particularly hurtful or insulting, and which the person who is apologizing should promise never to do again. Saying "I'm useless as a parent" does not commit a person to any specific improvement.

These pseudo-apologies are used by people who believe saying sorry shows weakness, Parents who wish to teach their children to apologize should see it as a sign of strength, and therefore not resort to these pseudo-apologies.

But even when presented with examples of genuine contrition, children still need help to become a ware of the complexities of saying sorry. A three-year-old might need help in understanding that other children feel pain just as he does, and that hitting a playmate over the head with a heavy toy requires an apology. A six-year-old might need reminding that spoiling other children's expectations can require an apology. A 12-year-old might need to be shown that raiding the biscuit tin without asking permission is acceptable, but that borrowing a parent's clothes without permission is not.

1. If a mother adds "but" to an apology, _____.

   A) she doesn't feel that she should have apologized

   B) she does not realize that the child has been hurt

   C) the child may find the apology easier to accept

   D) the child may feel that he owes her an apology

2. According to the author, saying "I'm sorry you're upset" most probably means "_____".

   A) You have good reason to get upset

   B) I'm aware you're upset, but I'm not to blame

   C) I apologize for hurting your feelings

   D) I'm at fault for making you upset

3. It is not advisable to use the general, all-covering apology because _____.

   A) it gets one into the habit of making empty promises

   B) it may make the other person feel guilty

   C) it is vague and ineffective

   D) it is hurtful and insulting

4. We learn from the last paragraph that in teaching children to say sorry
   _____.

   A）the complexities involved should be ignored

   B）their ages should be taken into account

   C）parents need to set them a good example

   D）parents should be patient and tolerant

5. It can be inferred from the passage that apologizing properly is _____.

   A）a social issue calling for immediate attention

   B）not necessary among family members

   C）a sign of social progress

   D）not as simple as it seems

解析：

1. D）。孩子会认为他欠她一个道歉。在文章中第二段最后提到"只会让已经受了伤害的人再次感觉到在等待道歉的同时，他们应就自己欠妥的行为表示歉意"。

2. B）。我知道你不高兴了，但是我没有责怪你。通过题目的问题，可以在文章中的第三段找到，句子的后面强调"这句话表明你感觉自己有错，因为你让自己的情绪受到别人的影响而变得不好了"。因此答案为 B。

3. C）。这样的道歉比较含糊或者是没什么效果。通过题目中的 all-covering apology 可以在文章中第四段找到，而最后一句话强调到"我不是很称职的父母并不表明一个人会做任何的改进"。也就是说这种道歉没有什么效果。

4. B）。需要考虑到他们的年纪。问题是"最后一段在教育孩子上说对不起——"直接定位在最后一段"But even when presented with examples of genuine contrition, children still need help to become aware of the complexities of saying sorry." 说明"即使在父母已经举例阐述自己真心忏悔以后，小孩还是需要家长的帮助来体会道歉的复杂"。接着举了 3 个不同年龄段的小孩分别要对哪些行为道歉。

5. D)。并不是像看上去那样简单。本题为概括题，从上一题的分析，可以得知体会道歉是很复杂的，并没有像我们想象中的那么简单。

测评：

题　型　正误题数	正确题数	错误题数
选择题		
正确率		
备注：正确率达80%以上为优秀，70%以上为良好，60%以上为合格		

▶**Passage two**

Can electricity cause cancer? In a society that literally runs on electric power, the very idea seems preposterous. But for more than a decade, a growing band of scientists and journalists has pointed to studies that seem to link exposure to electromagnetic fields with increased risk of leukemia and other malignancies. The implications are unsettling, to say the least, since everyone comes into contact with such fields, which are generated by everything electrical, from power lines and antennas to personal computers and micro-wave ovens. Because evidence on the subject is inconclusive and often contradictory, it has been hard to decide whether concern about the health effects of electricity is legitimate — or the worst kind of paranoia.

Now the alarmists have gained some qualified support from the U. S. Environmental Protection Agency. In the executive summary of a new scientific review, released in draft form late last week, the EPA has put forward what amounts to the most serious government warning to date. The agency tentatively concludes that scientific evidence "suggests a casual link" between extremely low-frequency electromagnetic fields — those having very longwave-lengths — and leukemia, lymphoma and brain cancer, While the report falls short of classifying ELF fields as probable carcinogens, it does identify the common 60-hertz magnetic field as "a possible, but not proven, cause of cancer in humans."

The report is no reason to panic — or even to lost sleep. If there is a cancer risk, it is a small one. The evidence is still so controversial that the draft stirred a great deal of debate within the Bush Administration, and the EPA released it over strong objections from the Pentagon and the White House. But now no one can deny that the issue must be taken seriously and that much more research is needed.

At the heart of the debate is a simple and well-understood physical phenomenon: When an electric current passes through a wire, which generates an electromagnetic field that exerts forces on surrounding objects, For many years, scientists dismissed any suggestion that such forces might be harmful, primarily because they are so extraordinarily weak. The ELF magnetic field generated by a video terminal measures only a few milligauss, or about one-hundredth the strength of the earth's own magnetic field, The electric fields surrounding a power line can be as high as 10 kilovolts per meter, but the corresponding field induced in human cells will be only about 1 millivolt per meter. This is far less than the electric fields that the cells themselves generate.

How could such minuscule forces pose a health danger? The consensus used to be that they could not, and for decades scientists concentrated on more powerful kinds of radiation, like X-rays, that pack sufficient wallop to knock electrons out of the molecules that make up the human body. Such "ionizing" radiations have been clearly linked to increased cancer risks and there are regulations to control emissions.

But epidemiological studies, which find statistical associations between sets of data, do not prove cause and effect. Though there is a body of laboratory work showing that exposure to ELF fields can have biological effects on animal tissues, a mechanism by which those effects could lead to cancerous growths has never been found.

The Pentagon is from persuaded. In a blistering 33-page critique of the EPA report, Air Force scientists charge its authors with having "biased the entire document" toward proving a link. "Our reviewers are convinced that there is no suggestion that (electromagnetic fields) present in the environment induce or promote cancer," the Air Force concludes. "It is astonishing that the EPA would lend its imprimatur on this report." Then Pentagon's concern is understandable. There is hardly a unit of the modern military that does not depend on the heavy use of some kind of electronic equipment, from huge ground-based radar towers to the defense systems built into every warship and plane.

1. The main idea of this passage is _____.

    A) studies on the cause of cancer

    B) controversial view-points in the cause of cancer

    C) the relationship between electricity and cancer

    D) different ideas about the effect of electricity on caner

2. The view-point of the EPA is _____.

    A) there is casual link between electricity and cancer

    B) electricity really affects cancer

    C) controversial

    D) low frequency electromagnetic field is a possible cause of cancer

3. Why did the Pentagon and Whit House object to the release of the report? Because _____.

    A) it may stir a great deal of debate among the Bush Administration.

    B) every unit of the modern military has depended on the heavy use of some kind of electronic equipment

    C) the Pentagon's concern was understandable

    D) they had different arguments

4. It can be inferred from physical phenomenon _____.

    A) the force of the electromagnetic field is too weak to be harmful

    B) the force of the electromagnetic field is weaker than the electric field that the cells generate

C）electromagnetic field may affect health

D）only more powerful radiation can knock electron out of human body

5. What do you think ordinary citizens may do after reading the different arguments?

A）They are indifferent.

B）They are worried very much.

C）The may exercise prudent avoidance.

D）They are shocked.

答 案　D　A　B　A　C

解析：

1. 选 D）。电力对癌症影响的不同观点。文章一开始就提出了"电会致癌吗？"这个问题。十多年来，一大批科学家和新闻界人士都指出：研究结果似乎表示接触电磁场可能会增加患白血病和其他恶性肿瘤的危险性。所以说到目前为止还难以确定电对健康的影响究竟是理性的，还是杞人忧天。第二段公布了环保署的报告，第三段说明：即使有致癌危险也是极微的。但应予以认真对待，进行更多的研究。而第七段中五角大楼还没有被说服，明确提出，我们的评论员认为没有迹象说明环境中存在的电力会诱发或促发癌症。

A）对致癌因素的研究；B）致癌原因方面有争议的观点，这两项根本不对，和文内电力毫无关系；C）电力和癌症的关系，文中涉及的是电力究竟会不会致癌的两种观点，而不是两者的关系。

2. 选 A）。电和致癌有一定难以确定的关系。答案在第二段第三句，环保署目前的结论是根据科学证据指出极低频电磁场——具有长波的电磁场——和白血病、淋巴瘤及脑癌之间有着难以确定的联系。

B）电确实致癌，不对；C）有争议的，说的不够清楚，争议什么；D）低频磁场是一个可能致癌因素，这只是论点的一面。

3. 选 B）。现代军事的任何部门都一直依赖于大量应用电子设备。五角大楼和白宫所以反对环保署公布报告的理由就在此。空军方面的专家所以说环保署方面的报告"歪曲了整个文件以证明两者之间的关系"也在此。所以文内说"五角大楼的关注是可以理解的。"

A）报告会在布什政府内引起大规模的辩论，这是结果；C）五角大楼的关注是可以理解的，这不是原因；D）他们有不同的观点。

4. 磁场力太弱不会产生有害作用。答案在第四段第二、第三句，当电流通过电缆，产生磁场，对周围物体产生（影响）力。许多年来，科学家把任何有关"这些力可能有害的想法"置于一边（不予考虑），主要是因为它们（所产生的力）非常弱。

B）磁场力比细胞产生的电磁场弱，只是明确指出的事实；C）磁场力对人的健康有害，不对；D）只有更强的辐射才能把人体中的电子击出来，不对。

5. 选 C）。他们会尽量谨慎小心的避开和电器接触。因为他们不可能像 A 项那样漠不关心。这种问题直接影响人的生命。

B）他们非常担忧；D）他们感到震惊，这两项都不可能，因为还在争议中，唯一的途径是尽量避开和电器接触。

测评：

题　型＼正误题数	正确题数	错误题数
选择题		
正确率		

备注：正确率达 80% 以上为优秀，70% 以上为良好，60% 以上为合格

▶**Passage Three**

Yet the difference in tome and language must strike us, so soon as it is philosophy that speaks: that change should remind us that even if the function of religion and that of reason coincide, this function is performed in the two cases by very different organs. Religions are many, reason one. Religion consists of conscious ideas, hopes, enthusiasms, and objects of worship; it operates by grace and flourishes by prayer. Reason, on the other hand, is a mere principle or potential order, on which indeed we may come to reflect but which exists in us ideally only, without variation or stress of any kind. We conform or do not conform to it; it does not urge or chide us, not call for any emotions on our part other than those naturally aroused by the various objects which it unfolds in their true nature and proportion. Religion brings some order into life by weighting it with new materials. Reason adds to the natural materials only the perfect order which it introduces into them. Rationality is nothing but a form, an ideal constitution which experience may more or less embody. Religion is a part of experience itself, a mass of sentiments and ideas. The one is an inviolate principle, the other a changing and struggling force. And yet this struggling and changing force of religion seems to direct man toward something eternal. It seems to make for an ultimate harmony within the soul and for an ultimate harmony between the soul and all that the soul depends upon. Religion, in its intent, is a more conscious and direct pursuit of the Life of Reason than is society, science, or art, for these approach and fill out the ideal life tentatively and piecemeal, hardly regarding the foal or caring for the ultimate justification of the instinctive aims. Religion also has an instinctive and blind side and bubbles up in all manner of chance practices and intuitions; soon, however, it feels its way toward the heart of things, and from whatever quarter it may come, veers in the direction of the ultimate.

Nevertheless, we must confess that this religious pursuit of the Life of Reason has been singularly abortive. Those within the pale of each religion may prevail upon themselves, to express satisfaction with its results, thanks to a fond partiality in reading the past and generous draughts of hope for the future; but any one regarding the various religions at once and comparing their achievements with what reason requires, must feel how terrible is the disappointment which they have one and all prepared for mankind. Their chief anxiety has been to offer imaginary remedies for mortal ills, some of which are incurable essentially, while others might have been really cured by well-directed effort. The Greed oracles, for instance, pretended to heal out natural ignorance, which has its appropriate though difficult cure, while the Christian vision of heaven pretended to be an antidote to our natural death-the inevitable correlate of birth and of a changing and conditioned existence. By methods of this sort little can be done for the real betterment of life. To confuse intelligence and dislocate sentiment by gratuitous fictions is a short-sighted way of pursuing happiness. Nature is soon avenged. An unhealthy exaltation and a one-sided morality have to be followed by regrettable reactions. When these come. The real rewards of life may seem vain to a relaxed vitality, and the very name of virtue may irritate young spirits untrained in and natural excellence. Thus religion too often debauches the morality it comes to sanction and impedes the science it ought to fulfill.

What is the secret of this ineptitude? Why does religion, so near to rationality in its purpose, fall so short of it in its results? The answer is easy; religion pursues rationality through the imagination. When it explains events or assigns causes, it is an imaginative substitute for science. When it gives precepts, insinuates ideals, or remoulds aspiration, it is an imaginative substitute for wisdom — I mean for the deliberate and impartial pursuit of all food. The condition and the aims of life are both represented in religion poetically, but this poetry tends to arrogate to itself literal truth and moral authority, neither of which it possesses. Hence the depth and importance of religion becomes intelligible no less than its contradictions and practical disasters. Its object is the same as that of reason, but its method is to proceed by intuition and by unchecked poetical conceits.

1. As used in the passage, the author would define "wisdom" as _____.

   A) the pursuit of rationality through imagination

   B) an unemotional search for the truth

   C) a purposeful and unbiased quest for what is best

   D) a short-sighted way of pursuing happiness

2. Which of the following statements is NOT TRUE?

　　A）Religion seeks the truth through imagination, reason, in its search, utilizes the emotions.

　　B）Religion has proved an ineffective tool in solving man's problems.

　　C）Science seeks a piece meal solution to man's questions.

　　D）The functions of philosophy and reason are the same.

3. According to the author, science differs from religion in that _____.

　　A）it is unaware of ultimate goals

　　B）it is unimaginative

　　C）its findings are exact and final

　　D）it resembles society and art

4. The author states that religion differs from rationality in that _____.

　　A）it relies on intuition rather than reasoning

　　B）it is not concerned with the ultimate justification of its instinctive aims

　　C）it has disappointed mankind

　　D）it has inspired mankind

5. According to the author, the pursuit of religion has proved to be _____.

　　A）imaginative

　　B）a provider of hope for the future

　　C）a highly intellectual activity

　　D）ineffectual

答案 C A A D D

解析：

1. 选 C）。一种有目的而又不带偏见对事物最佳的探索。答案在最后一段，宗教是通过想象来追逐理性，当它解释事件或阐明原因时，以虚构的想象来取代科学，当它训诫，暗示理想或者重塑抱负时，以想象代替智慧——智慧的意思是指有意识而又公正的追求一切好东西。

A）通过想象力追求理性；B）不带感情的探询真理；C）追求幸

福的短视的方法。

2. 选 A）。宗教通过想象力寻求真理，而理性的探索却运用感情。理性（智）是非感情的。B）在解决人类问题上的宗教是一种无效的工具；C）科学寻求逐步解决对人类的问题；D）哲学和理性的功能是一样的。

3. 选 A）。宗教没有意识（不知道）其最终目的的。说明宗教不管（几乎不关注）其目的，或不关心其本能的目标最终正确与否。B）宗教没有想象力；C）其成果是确切的，最终的；D）宗教很象科学和艺术。

4. 选 D）。它激起人类情感。第一段中说"宗教的挣扎与不断变化的力量似乎促使人追求某种永恒的东西，它似乎追求灵魂的最终和谐以及灵魂与灵魂所依赖的一起事物之间的永恒的和谐。"A. 宗教依赖于直觉而不是推理，第一段最后一句：宗教也有本能和盲目的一面，在各种各样的偶然实践和直觉中沸腾，可不久它又向事物内心摸索前进，然而不论从哪个方向来，都转向最终方向（最终多转向这个方向——直觉），文章的最后一句：宗教的目的和理想的目的一样，而其实现目的的方法是通过直觉和无限止的诗一般的幻想来进行的；B）它不关心其本能的目标最终是否正确；C）它使人类很失望。

5. 选 D）。无效。第二段开始就点出：我们得承认宗教追求理性生活一直是很失败（流产了）。

A）有想象力的；B）为未来提供希望的；C）是一个高度的智力活动。

测评：

题　型 ＼ 正误题数	正确题数	错误题数
选择题		
正确率		
备注：正确率达 80% 以上为优秀，70% 以上为良好，60% 以上为合格		

▶Passage Four

Cryptic coloring is by far the commonest use of color in the struggle for existence. It is employed for the purpose of attack (aggressive resemblance or anticryptic coloring) as well as of defense (protective resemblance or procryptic coloring). The fact that the same method concealment, may be used both for attack and defense has been well explained by T. Belt who suggests as an illustration the rapidity of movement which is also made use of by both pursuer and pursued, which is similarly raised to a maximum in both by the gradual dying out of the slowest through a series of generations. Cryptic coloring is commonly associated with other aids in the struggle for life. Thus well-concealed mammals and birds, when discovered, will generally endeavor to escape by speed and will often attempt to defend themselves actively. On the other hand, small animals which have no means of active defense, such as large, numbers of insects, frequently depend upon concealment alone. Protective resemblance is far commoner among animals than aggressive resemblance, in correspondence with the fact that predaceous forms are as a rule much larger and much less numerous than their prey. In the case of insectivorous Vertebrata and their prey such differences exist in an exaggerated form. Cryptic coloring, whether used for defense of attack, may be either general or special. In general resemblance the animal, in consequence of its coloring, produces the same effect as its environment, but the conditions do not require any special adaptation of shape and outline. General resemblance is especially common among the animal inhabiting some uniformly colored expanse of the earth's surface, such as an ocean or a desert. In the former, animals of all shapes are frequently protected by their transparent blue color, on the latter, equally diverse forms are defended by their sandy appearance. The effect of a uniform appearance may be produced by a combination of tints in startling contrast. Thus the black and white stripes of the zebra blend together at a little distance, and "their proportion is such as exactly to match the pale tint which arid ground possesses when seen by moonlight." Special resemblance is far commoner than general and is the form which is usually met with on the diversified surface of the earth, on the shores, and in shallow water, as well as on the floating masses of algae on the surface of the ocean, such as the Sargasso Sea. In these environments the cryptic coloring of animals is usually aided by special modifications of shape, and by the instinct which leads them to assume particular attitudes. Complete stillness and the assumption of a certain attitude play an essential part in general resemblance on land; but in special resemblance the attitude is often highly specialized, and perhaps more important than any other element in the complex method by which concealment is effected. In special resemblance the combination of coloring, shape, and attitude is such as to produce a more or less exact resemblance to some one of the objects in the environment, such as a leaf of twig, a patch of lichen, a flake of bark. In all cases the resemblance is to some object which is of no interest to the enemy or prey respectively. The animal is not hidden from view by becoming indistinguishable from its background as in the case of general resemblance, but it is mistaken for some well-know object.

In seeking the interpretation of these most interesting and elaborate adaptations, attempts have been made along two lines. The first seeks to explain the effect as a result of the direct influence of the environment upon the individual (G. L. L. Buffon), or by the inherited effects of efforts and the use and disuse of parts (J. B. P. Lamarck). The second believes that natural selection produced the result and afterwards maintained it by the survival of the best concealed in each generation. The former suggestion breaks down when the complex nature of numerous special resemblances is appreciated. Thus the arrangement of colors of many kinds into an appropriate pattern requires the cooperation of a suitable shape and the rigidly exact adoption of a certain elaborate attitude. The latter is instinctive and thus depends on the central nervous system. The cryptic effect is due to the exact cooperation of all these factors; and in the present state of science, the only possible hole of an interpretation lies in the theory of natural selection, which can accumulate any and every variation which tends toward survival. A few of the chief types of methods by which concealment is effected may be briefly described. The colors of large numbers of vertebrate animals are darkest on the back and become gradually lighter on the sides, passing into white on the belly. Abbot H. Thayer has suggested that this gradation obliterates the appearance of solidity, which is due to shadow. The color harmony, which is also essential to concealment, is produced because the back is of the same tint as the environment (e. g. earth), bathed in the cold blue-white of the sky, while the belly, being cold blue-white and bathed in shadow and yellow earth reflections produces the same effects. This method of neutralizing shadow for the purpose of concealment by increased lightness of tint was first suggested by E. B. Poulton in the case of a larva and a pupa, but he did not appreciate the great importance of the principle. In an analogous method an animal in front of a background of dark shadow may have part of its body obliterated by the existence of a dark tint, the remainder resembling, e. g. , a part of a leaf. This method of rendering invisible any part which would interfere with the resemblance is well know in mimicry.

1. The black and white stripes of the zebra are most useful form of

_____ .

   A) hunters   B) nocturnal predators

   C) lions and tigers   D) insectivorous Vertrbrata

2. Aggressive resemblance occurs when _____ .

   A) a predaceous attitude is assumed

   B) special resemblance is utilized

   C) an animal relies on speed

D) an animal blends in with its background

3. Special resemblance differs from general resemblance in that the animal relies on _____ .

   A) its ability to frighten its adversary

   B) speed

   C) its ability to assume an attitude

   D) mistaken identify

4. The title below that best expresses the ides of this passage is _____ .

   A) cryptic coloration for Protection

   B) how Animals Survive

   C) the uses of Mimicry in Nature

   D) resemblances of Animals

5. Of the following which is the least common?

   A) Protective resemblance.   B) General resemblance.

   C) Aggressive resemblance.   D) Special resemblance.

答 案 1. B 2. A 3. D 4. C 5. C

解析:

1. 选 B)。夜间活动的食肉动物。斑马黑白相间颜色的比例正好和月光下所见的贫瘠土地苍白的色泽相吻合。当然能保护斑马夜间免遭这些食肉动物的袭击。

   A) 捕获者;C) 狮子和老虎;D) 食虫的脊椎动物。

2. 选 A)。在装备捕食其他动物的姿势时。B) 应该专门模仿;C) 动物依赖速度;D) 动物和背景混在一起。

3. 选 D)。搞错/认错了动物(身份)(mistaken identify 认错了人之意)。见第一段最后一句话,它不像一般模仿那样,通过动物和背景难以辨别从而在视觉中隐藏起来,它被误认为某种著名动物。A) 用以吓走它的对手(敌人)的能力;B) 速度;C) 采用某种姿势的能力。

4. 选 C)。自然界模拟的运动。文章一开始就说保护色是迄今为止生存斗争中最常用的一种颜色,常用于进攻和防卫。保护色常和其他措施相配合，首先提到速度，然后讲到保护色分类，一般（普通）和特殊（专门）模拟/模仿。第二段解释或说明模拟适应性。第一种解释为环境使然/影响。第二种认为是自然界选择之结果。

A）为了保卫的保护色；B）动物是如何存活下来的；D）动物之模仿性。

5. 选 C）。进攻性（侵犯性）模仿。

A）保护色模仿；B）一般性模仿；D）专项模仿。

测评：

题 型　　正误题数	正确题数	错误题数
选择题		
正确率		

备注：正确率达80%以上为优秀，70%以上为良好，60%以上为合格

▶Passage Five

How could faith beget such evil? After hundreds of members of a Ugandan cult, the Movement for the Restoration of the Ten Commandments of God, died in what first appeared to be a suicidal fire in the village of Kanungu two weeks age, police found 153 bodies buried in a compound used by the cult in Buhunga, 25 miles away. When investigators searched the house of a cult leader in yet another village, they discovered 155 bodies, many buried under the concrete floor of the house. Then scores more were dug up at a cult member's home. Some had been poisoned; others, often-young children, strangled. By week's end, Ugandan police had counted 924 victims — including at least 530 who burned to death inside the sealed church — exceeding the 1978 Jonestown mass suicide and killings by followers of American cult leader Jim Jones that claimed 913 lives.

Authorities believe two of the cult's leaders, Joseph Kibwetere, a 68-year-old former Roman Catholic catechism teacher who started the cult in 1987, and his "prophetess," Credonia Mwerinde, by some accounts a former prostitute who claimed to speak for the Virgin Mary, may still be alive and on the run. The pair had predicted the world would end on Dec. 31, 1999. When that didn't happen, followers who demanded the return of their possessions, which they had to surrender on joining the cult, may have been systematically killed.

The Ugandan carnage focuses attention on the proliferation of religious cults in East Africa's impoverished rural areas and city slums. According to the institute for the study of American religion, which researches cults and sects, there are now more than 5,000 indigenous churches in Africa, some with apocalyptic or revolutionary leanings. One such group is the Jerusalem Church of Christ in Nairobi's Kawangwara slums, led by Mary Snaida-Akatsa, or "mommy" as she is known to her thousands of followers. She prophesies about the end of the world and accuses some members of being witches. One day they brought a "special visitor" to church, an Indian Sikh man she claimed was Jesus, and told her followers to "repent or pay the consequences."

Most experts say Africa's hardships push people to seek hope in religious cults. "These groups thrive because of poverty," says Charles Onyango Obbo, editor of the Monitor, an independent newspaper in Uganda, and a close observer of cults. "People have no support, and they're susceptible to anyone who is able to tap into their insecurity." Additionally, they say, AIDS, which has ravaged East Africa, may also breed a fatalism that helps apocalyptic notions take root.

Some Africans turn to cults after rejecting mainstream Christian churches as "Western" or "non-African." Agnes Masitsa, 30, who used to attend a Catholic church before she joined the Jerusalem Church of Christ, says of Catholicism: "It's dull."

Catholic icons, the Ugandan doomsday cult, like many of the sects, drew on features of Roman Catholicism, a strong force in the region. Catholic icons were prominent in its buildings, and some of its leaders were defrocked priests, such as Dominic Kataribabo, 32, who reportedly studied theology in the Los Angeles area in the mid-1980s. He had told neighbors he was digging a pit in his house to install a refrigerator; police have now recovered 81 bodies from under the floor and 74 from a field nearby. Police are unsure whether Kataribabo died in the church fire.

Still, there is the question: How could so many killings have been carried out without drawing attention? Villagers were aware of Kibwetere's sect, whose followers communicated mainly through sign language and apparently were apprehensive about violating any of the cult's commandments. There were suspicions. Ugandan president Yoweri Mseveni told the BBC that intelligence reports about the dangerous nature of the group had been suppressed by some government officials. On Thursday, police arrested an assistant district commissioner, the Rev. Amooti Mutazindwa, for allegedly holding back a report suggesting the cult posed a security threat.

Now, there are calls for African governments to monitor cults more closely. Says Gilbert Ogutu, a professor of religious studies at the University of Nairobi: "When cult leaders lose support, they become dangerous."

1. Why did so many Ugandans die in faith?

   A) Many of them were killed for asking for the return of their possessions.

   B) They found the cult's leaders had cheated them.

   C) They lost faith in cults.

   D) They are willing to die.

2. The main reason of people's joining the cults is _____.

   A) poverty   B) insecurity   C) AIDS   D) fatalism

3. What does Mary Snaide Akatsa prophesy?

   A) She prophesies the world will be flooded.

   B) She prophesies the world will be in fire.

C）She prophesies about the end of the world.

D）She prophesies he followers should die in faith.

4. Why do some Africans reject Christian Churches?

A）They feel Christianity is dull.

B）They reject Christian Churches as Western or non-African.

C）They are susceptible.

D）They are dangerous persons.

5. How could so many killing have been carried out without drawing attention?

A）The cult acted secretly.

B）The government officials did not see through its dangerous nature.

C）There were no preventive measures.

D）People were frightened.

答案　1. A　2. A　3. C　4. B　5. A

解析:

1. 选 A）。许多人由于要归还他们的财产而遭到杀害。答案见第二段倒数第二句，这一对邪教领袖曾预言世界将于 1999 年 12 月 31 日借宿——世界末日来临。结果并没有发生，追随者就要求归还他们在入教时献上的一切，而遭到有计划有步骤地杀害。

　B）他们发现邪教头目欺骗他们，这只是起因之一，如果发现后不吭声也许不会有事；C）他们对邪教失去了信任；D）他们愿意去死。

2. 选 A）。贫穷。主要原因就是穷。答案见第四段。许多专家认为非洲的艰苦生活促使人民在邪教中寻找希望。这些邪教群体的兴起就是因为贫穷。人民没有支柱、保障，很容易受影响。任何人都可利用他们不安的情绪。其次艾滋病在东非的猖獗，培育出宿命论观点，从而帮助预示可怕事情即将来临的思想扎根于心灵。

　B）不安全；C）艾滋病；D）宿命论。

3. 选 C）。她预言世界末日。

　A）她预言世界将遭水淹；B）她预言世界将烧光；D）她预言她

的追随者将死于信仰。

4. 选 B）。他们把基督教会视为西方的或非非洲的而拒之门外。见第五段：有些非洲人在把基督教会视作西方的或非非洲的而拒之门外后皈依邪教。

   A）认为基督教非常沉闷单调；C）他们易受影响；D）他们是一伙危险人物。

5. 选 A）。邪教行动神秘。例：第一段中描述的好几百乌干达邪教组织成员死于初看好像是自杀性的火焰之中（自焚），在一个场院又发现了 153 具尸体，在搜查邪教头目的房子中又发现了 156 具尸体，许多埋于房子的混凝土地板下面，还有好几十具从邪教成员家中挖出，其中有些人被毒死。其他，特别是孩子都是扼杀（窒息而死）。共计 924 人，至少有 530 人烧死在封闭的教堂里。倒数第三段，乌干达世界末日邪教一个头目——免去圣职的牧师，据说 20 世纪 80 年代中他研究神学，他告诉邻居他在家挖一个地窖放冰箱。现在警察发现地板下 81 具尸体，附近一场地发现 74 具尸体。上述两例都是神秘杀害，至于要归还财产之人更遭神秘杀害了。

   B）政府官员没有看出邪教的危险性（原因之一）；C）没有防范措施；D）人民害怕。

测评：

题　型　正误题数	正确题数	错误题数
选择题		
正确率		

备注：正确率达 80% 以上为优秀，70% 以上为良好，60% 以上为合格

第三章 CET-4 阅读解题技巧

第一节 快速阅读解题方法与答题技巧

一、快速阅读解题方法

快速阅读要求考生在15分钟内完成一篇1200个单词左右的文章和后面的10道题。前面7个题是判断正误（包括 NOT GIVEN），后3个是填空题（答案基本都是原文中出现的原词）。从文章的篇幅和题目的设置都让我们感觉到，考生在复习阶段必须有意识地培养快速阅读能力，以便有效地应对这个部分的测试。

2007年12月新四级考试的快速阅读部分已经由原来的 Y、N、NG 变为4选1的多项选择题了。新题型与原来的相比变化不大，只是回答问题的方式换了一下。

快速阅读能力的提高固然有赖于考生在大量阅读中逐步的积累。但是，在平时训练的时候，应该注意通过对逻辑关系、标点符号、一些特征语言信息点，乃至寻读等方法的积极运用，实现文章主旨的快速把握，并对随后的题目作出有效的判断和填写。

（一）逻辑关系在快速阅读中的运用

快速阅读理解能力的提高是有一定方法可循的，为此我们首先提示考生应该尤其注意文章逻辑关系在快速阅读中的运用。逻辑关系散布在文章的句子内部、句句之间以及段落之间。最基本的逻辑关系有以下几种：

（1）因果关系：as a result, therefore, hence, consequently, because, for, due to, hence, consequently 等。

（2）并列、递进关系：and, or, then, in addition, besides, in

other words，moreover 等。

（3）转折关系：however，but，yet，in fact 等。

这些我们其实已经很熟悉的逻辑提示词在文章中起的效果，并非仅仅是衔接文章的句子，从阅读的角度来看，其实同时在给我们某种提示，告诉我们哪些句子是有效信息，相对重要的信息，哪些信息是相对不重要的信息，因为我们在处理文章的时候，有一条清晰的思路，你不是为了完整翻译文章而进行阅读，而是为了获取主旨来阅读。

相应地，并列、递进关系词，意味着它们前后衔接的信息从主旨的体现上没有发生变化，而更多的表现为前后句子主旨的相似性，所以我们选择其中的一半进行阅读。这样，在保证了阅读质量的基础上，也极大地提高了阅读速度。

（二）标点符号在快速阅读中的运用

可以运用标点符号（破折号、小括号、冒号）了解不认识的词汇或句子的含义。因为这些标点符号的出现就是为了更进一步地了解和认识之前的信息。但同时，由于快速阅读用词相对比较简单，很容易理解和把握标点前的被解释信息，所以，可以将这些标点符号后面的信息删除，从而更加快速地把握文章的主旨。

例如样题中有下列信息：

· Dump — an open hole in the ground where trash is buried and that is full of various animals（rats，mice，birds）.（This is most people's idea of a landfill！）

· Landfill — carefully designed structure built into or on top of the ground in which trash is isolated from the surrounding environment（groundwater，air，rain）. This isolation is accomplished with a bottom liner and daily covering of soil.

· Sanitary landfill — land fill that uses a clay liner to isolate the trash from the environment

· Municipal solid waste（MSW）landfill — landfill that uses a synthetic（plastic）liner to isolate the trash from the environment

注意到在"Dump"、"Landfill"之后分别有一个破折号，如果我们已经明白该标点的意义就在于后面的信息对前者进一步进行解释，那么就可以在明白这些单词基本含义的基础上，放弃其后信息的阅读，因为，阅读理解，我们更强调的是对文章主旨信息的把握，而不是具体的细节信息。

（三）特殊信息点在快速阅读中的运用

所谓"特殊信息点"是指那些很容易在文章中识别的词汇，诸如时间、数字、大写字母等形式的语言点。这些形式的表达一方面很容易识别出来，另一方面，这些信息点表现的一般都是文章的琐碎信息，对于主旨的理解和把握而言，不过是更进一步论证而已。因此，可以忽略这些信息的阅读。如果后面测试的题点中确实涉及到了，再回来细读也无妨，毕竟它们的表现形式非常利于查找和定位判断。

（四）寻读在快速阅读中的运用

寻读的目的主要是有目标地去找出文中某些特定的信息，也就是说，在对文章有所了解（即略读）后，在文章中查找与某一问题、某一观点或某一单词有关的信息，寻找解题的可靠依据。寻读时，要以很快的速度扫视文章，确定所查询的信息范围。值得庆幸的是，在大学英语四级快速阅读的测试文章中，已经有了明确的小标题，这就能够帮助我们很快地锁定解题范围。同时，还应该注意题目中体现出的所查信息的特点。如：问题或填空的句子中涉及到人名、地名，则主要寻找首字母大写的单词；有关日期、数目的问题，则主要查找具体数字；有关某个事件、某种观点等，就需要寻找与此相关的关键词，而与所查信息无关的内容可一掠而过。

总的来说，从最新的样题来看，快速阅读理解部分由于其篇幅长，题目灵活，会让考生感觉无从下手。但是，对于该题型我们有一个清晰的概念，那就是快速阅读测试的重点就是考生在短时间内获取篇章主旨和特定信息的能力，因此，它更强调了正确的阅读方法和技巧的贯彻。只要我们掌握一定的方法，培养好的阅读习惯，还是很容易在一段时间内取得快速进步的。

二、答题技巧

针对快速阅读，我们总结了如下答题技巧：

（1）把没用的信息跳过。想找到有用的信息，先要知道你要什么信息，才能有的放矢。要记住尽量少但最有效的问题单词或者句子。要找这样的单词：原文当中出现而且题目也出现，这样的单词是重点，文章出现这样单词的前后要着重读，很可能答案就在这。

（2）如果你找不到这样的单词，就要看懂问题问的是什么，然后带着这个问题在读文章的时候要有目的的读，遇到了就要仔细的读，很可能问题答案就在那附近。

（3）如果以上两点你都没办法确定，那就要注意文章的首末句子，首末段落，按照经验来说，这些地方出现答案的机会还是最多的。

（4）大家在平时做英语阅读训练的时候，要定好时间训练，多练习就会适应快速阅读了，而且还能找到做题的技巧。

（5）大家还是要增强英语基础词汇和语法的练习，没有一定的词汇量，任何技巧都无法实现它应有的效果。

第二节 篇章词汇阅读与简答解题方法与答题技巧

一、篇章词汇解题方法和答题技巧

对于如何抓住整篇文章的重点，应掌握以下几点：

1. 跳读全文，抓住中心

首先考生应该跳读全文，根据首段原则以及首末句原则，迅速抓出文章的主题。判定文章主题对于篇章的整体把握具有很大的积极意义。

2. 阅读选项，词性分类

接着我们要仔细阅读选项。因为选项给我们的仅仅是一个单词，而非句子或者语段，所以考试难度就大大下降了。我们应该根据词性把每个单词进行分类归纳。如名词、动词、形容词、副词、介词、连词各有几个选项。

3. 瞻前顾后，灵活选择

然后我们在选择时，可以根据空格中应填入的词性，大大缩小选择范围。根据上下文的内在逻辑结构选择合适的选项填空。

4. 复读全文，谨慎调整

填空完成后，再次复读全文，自我感觉上下文是否通顺、内在逻辑关系是否连贯。如有问题，也需要谨慎地微作调整。

对于词的分析理解应注意的问题：

（1）判定词性时可以重点分析动词的时态，即哪几个是一般时，哪几个是过去时又或者是过去分词。因为根据样题，它对考生不做选项改写要求，所以我们可以根据上下文时态对应的原则，给自己进一步缩小选择范围。

（2）如果选项中出现指代词时，往往该选项不能放在首句，要注意指代成立的条件。

（3）如果选项中出现一组反义词时，往往有一个是干扰选项，它注重考察的是对于文章框架结构的理解，要求考生理解整篇文章的语境色彩。

（4）如果选项中出现一组近义词时，往往也有一个是干扰选项，它注重考察的是词汇的精确理解，要求考生分析清楚其细微的区别。

（5）如果选项为连词时，要关注上下句内在的逻辑关系。常见的逻辑关系有因果、并列平行、递进、强对比、前后意思一致等。

（6）要有总体观，不必按顺序作题。先把自己最有把握的词选出，然后删除该选项，为吃不准的选项缩小选择范围。

二、简答题解题方法和答题技巧

简答题常见题型有以下四类。

1. 细节类问题

由于简答题的宗旨在于重点考查考生的语言基本功及概括能力，所以一般来讲，简答题的细节类问题一般都能在原文中找到出处。

但关键是如何从答案出处中归纳出问题的答案，因为简答题要求考生既要用简短的语言，又不能原封不动地照搬原文的整句话，所以此类题看似简单，但要得满分也不是那么容易。

解答此类题型，首先要把答案找准，即找到问题中的关键词（线索词）在文章中的大体位置，并尽可能地缩小概括范围，然后再根据要求组织答案。

组织答案时，要注意以下几点：

（1）答案形式要符合提问方式。原文中提问方式为"why"，那么就用 Because 引导的从句回答。

（2）概括要简洁、准确，不要拖泥带水。

（3）注意语言表达符合语法。

2. 推断类试题

这种类型题目的答案在原文中是找不到的，它要求考生进行合理的推断，当然这种推断并非无源之水。文章中的某些用词、语气具有隐含意义（implied meaning），考生要做的只是将这种隐含意义读出来。

3. 主旨类试题

对于此类试题，第一步是找出概括文章中心思想的主题句，但主题句原文不能成为主旨题的答案，考生还需将主题句重新归纳总结。否则，照抄原句是要扣分的。然而，并不是所有的主旨类试题都能在原文中找到主题句。对于原文中没有提供主题句的主旨题，就需要考生概括对文章的理解，自己归纳总结答案。

4. 语意题

语意题的出题目的在于考查考生转述（paraphrase）或解释（explain）某个词或语句在特定场合下的特定含义的能力。该题型要求考生不仅要读懂原文，而且要表达出来。

解答这种题型时，可注意找出原词在文章中的同意代换词，如果没有，还应注意破折号、同位语从句、定语从句、插入句等具有解释、说明作用的语言成分。

注意大学英语四级考试的简答题关键在于：①看清题干；②注

意要求。回答问题中要切中要点，回答的形式还要同根据问题的形式相一致。

简答题需要注意的问题：①单数和复数的错误；②时态的错误；③不能重复题干；④不能照搬照抄原文，要去掉无效单词。

第三节　篇章阅读理解解题方法与答题技巧

一、篇章阅读解题方法

第一步：看文章后题目，分析定位词，并用笔标出以加深印象。

第二步：阅读文章。从头到尾把文章通读一遍，注意每段的中心句或中心思想，留心题目当中标出的信息；但是阅读的中途不要停顿下来去考虑单词、词组或句子的意思，不管懂还是不懂，一律跳过。

第三步：先做细节题，注意对比题目和文章当中相应信息在表述方式上的不同，要特别注意两者在用词上的区别——考的往往就是这个词！

第四步：在做完细节题并对于文章内容有了更深理解的基础之上完成主旨大意题，最佳标题题。篇章阅读可以细分为五类题目，主旨大意题、观点态度题、语意理解题、事实细节题和推理判断题。

二、篇章阅读答题技巧

1. 阅读时要辨别清楚文章的文体

议论文中，文章的中心句处一般暗示作者的态度；而说明文，因为其体裁的客观性，所以作者的态度也往往采取中立。在描叙性文章中，因为其文章观点往往不直接提出，而且作者写作时也常带有某种倾向性，所以，要求考生在读这种文体时要细心捕捉表达或暗示情感态度的词式短语，捕捉那些烘托气氛，渲染情感的词句。

2. 要理解文章中心思想

对于综合性判断情感态度的题，需要分析段落大意，分析文章走向，理解文章中心思想后才能判断出作者的情感态度来。

3. 要会区分不同的观点尤其要找出作者的观点

考生要注意文中出现的直接引语和间接语，出现的观点（一般是说话人而非作者的观点）。

在真正考试中应注意以下几点：

（1）如果第一段较短，可读完再看第一道题目，看能否做，如不能做，即问题在第一段中未提及，则接着往下读，读到能做为止。

如果第一段较长，则可读一半或一个层次后，找到中心句，看第一道题，看能否做，不能，接着读。

（2）以后几段，先看题后看文章，读一段做一题。如果题目涉及多段，则看完所有相关段落后，做题。

（3）近年来在阅读理解的文章中有时一题涉及多段，一段涉及多题。但每段的题目分配比较均匀。

此种方法的优点：易于精准定位，节省时间，提高正确率。

每篇文章最重要的就是第一段的第一句，最后一句；每段的第一句和最后一段的最后一句。因为这些往往是中心句，对于文章的思路、架构、作者的态度，有很强的说明性。

第四章 CET-4 阅读实战演练

第一节 快速阅读模拟训练——应试难度

特训一及答案

Media Selection for Advertisements

After determining the target audience for a product or service, advertising agencies must select the appropriate media for the advertisement. We discuss here the major types of media used in advertising. We focus our attention on seven types of advertising: television, newspapers, radio, magazines, out-of-home. Internet, and direct mail.

Television

Television is an attractive medium for advertising because it delivers mass audiences to advertisers. When you consider that nearly three out of four Americans have seen the game show Who Wants to Be a Millionaire? you can understand the power of television to communicate with a large audience. When advertisers create a brand, for example, they want to impress consumers with the brand and its image. Television provides an ideal vehicle for this type of communication. But television is an expensive medium, and not all advertisers can afford to use it.

Television's influence on advertising is fourfold. First, narrowcasting means that television channels are seen by an increasingly narrow segment of the audience. The Golf Channel, for instance, is watched by people who play golf. Home and Garden Television is seen by those interested in household improvement projects. Thus, audiences are smaller and more homogeneous（具有共同特点的）than they have been in the past. Second, there is an increase in the number of television channels available to viewers, and thus, advertisers. This has also resulted in an increase in the sheer number of advertisements to which audiences are exposed. Third, digital recording devices allow audience members more control over which commercials they watch. Fourth, control over programming is being passed from the networks to local cable operators and satellite programmers.

Newspaper

After television, the medium attracting the next largest annual ad revenue is newspapers. The New York Times, which reaches a national audience, accounts for $1 billion in ad revenue annually, im increased its national circulation（发行量）by 40% and is now available for home delivery in 168 cities. Locally, newspapers are the largest advertising medium.

Newspapers are a less expensive advertising medium than television and provide a way for advertisers to communicate a longer. more detailed message to their audience than they can through 48 hours, meaning newspapers are also a quick way of getting the massage out. Newspapers are ofen the most important form of news for a local community, and they develop a high degree of loyalty from local reader.

Radio

Advertising on radio continues to grow Radio is often used in conjunction with outdoor bill-boards（广告牌）and the Internet to reach even more customers than television. Advertisers are likely to use radio because it is a less expensive medium than television, which means advertisers can afford to repeal their ads often. Internet companies are also turning 10 radio advertising. Radio provides a way for advertisers to communicate with audience members at all times of the day. Consumers listen to radio on their way to school or work, at work, on the way home, and in the evening hours.

Two major changes — satellite and Internet radio — will force radio advertisers to adapt their methods. Both of these radio forms allow listeners to tune in stations that are more distant than the.

local stations they could receive in the past. As a result, radio will increasingly attract target audiences who live many miles apart.

Magazines

Newsweeklies, women's titles, and business magazines have all seen increases in advertising because they attract the high-end market, magazines are popular with advertisers because of the narrow market that they deliver. A broadcast medium such as network television attracts all types of audience members, but magazine audiences are more homogeneous. If you read sports illustrated, for example, you have much in common with the magazine's other readers. Advertisers see magazines as an efficient way of reaching target audience members.

Advertiser using the print media-magazines and newspapers-will need to adapt to two main changes. First, the internet will bring larger audiences to local newspapers, second. Advertisers will have to understand how to use an increasing number of magazines for their target audiences. Although some magazines will maintain national audiences, a large number of magazines will entertain narrower audiences.

Out-of-home advertising

Out-of-home advertising. Also called place-based advertising, has become an increasingly effective way of reaching consumers, who are more active than ever before. Many consumers today do not sit at home and watch television. Using billboards, newsstands, and bus shelters for advertising is an effective way of reaching these on-the-go consumers. More consumers travel longer distances to and from work, which also makes out-of-home advertising effective, technology has changed the nature of the billboard business, making it a more effective medium than in the past.

Using digital printing, billboard companies can print a billboard in 2 hours, compared with 6 days previously. This allows advertisers more variety in the types of messages they create because they. Can change their messages more quickly.

Internet

As consumers become more comfortable with online shopping, advertisers will seek to reach this market As consumers get more of their news and information from the Internet, the ability of television and radio to get the word out to consumers will decrease. The challenge to Internet advertisers is to create ads that audience members remember.

Internet advertising will play a more prominent role in organizations' advertising in the near ftuture. Internet audiences tend to be quite homogeneous, but small. Advertisers will have to adjust their methods to reach these audiences and will have to adapt their persuasive strategies to the online medium as well.

Direct mail

A final advertising medium is direct mail, which uses mailings to consumers to communicate a client's message Direct mail includes newsletters. postcards and special promotions. Direct mail is an effective way to build relationships with consumers. For many businesses. direct mail is the most effective from of advertising.

1. Television is an attractive advertising medium in that _____.

   A) it has large audiences

   B) it appeals to housewives

   C) it helps build up a company's reputation

   D) it is affordable to most advertiser

2. With the increase in the number of TV channels _____.

   A) the cost of TV advertising has decreased

   B) the nuiflber of TV viewers has increased

C）advertisers' interest in other media has decreased

D）the number of TV ads people can see has increased

3. Compared with television, newspapers as an advertising medium

_____ .

A）earn a larger annual ad revenue

B）convey more detailed messages

C）use more production techniques

D）get messages out more effectively

4. Advertising on radio continues to grow because _____ .

A）more local radio stations have been set up

B）modern technology makes it more entertaining

C）it provides easy access to consumers

D）it has been revolutionized by Internet radio

5. Magazines are seen by advertisers as an efficient way to _____ .

A）reach target audiences

B）modern technology makes it more entertaining

C）appeal to educated people

D）convey all kinds of messages

6. Out-of-home advertising has become more effective because _____ .

A）billboards can be replaced within two hours

B）consumers travel more now ever before

C）such ads have been made much more attractive

D）the pace of urban life is much faster nowadays

7. The challenge to Internet advertisers is to create ads that are _____ .

A）quick to update   B）pleasant to look at

C）easy to remember   D）convenient to access

8. Internet advertisers will have to adjust their methods to reach audiences that tend to be _____ .

9. Direct mail is an effecitve form of advertising for businesses to develop _____ .

10. This passage discusses how advertisers select _____ for

advertisements.

答案 1. A 2. D 3. B 4. D 5. A 6. A 7. D

8. adapted their persuaive strategies to the online medium as well

9. relalionships with consamens

10. the approprite media

特训二及答案

Getting Thin-for Good

Just about everyone has been on a diet at one time or another, and millions of us have learned that the weight we lose is all too easily regained. Still few people question the wisdom of dieting. After all, we reason, the worst that can happen is that we'll regain the weight we've lost-then we can simply go on a diet again.

But some new research suggests there is a risk: yo-yo dieting may seriously distort the body's weight-control system. The more diets you go on, the harder it may become to lose weight. Even worse, new evidence indicates that repeated cycles of losing and gaining weight may raise the risk of heart problems.

This last possibility is especially disturbing. As part of a 25-year study that monitored 1,959 men, researchers at the University of Texas School of Public Health in Houston reported in March 1987 that the men showing large up-and-down weight changes had twice the risk of heart disease as those with only small changes in weight. One paper from the Framingham (Mass.) Heart Study, which has monitored more than 5,000 people for 40 years, also provides troubling information: people who lost ten percent of their body weight had about 20 percent reduction in risk of heart disease-but people who gained 10 percent raised the risk by 30 percent. These numbers further suggest that going from 150 to 135 pounds, and back to 150 again, could leave you with a higher heart-disease risk than you started with.

When you cut calories and lose weight, your body will protect itself by reducing your basal metabolic rate (BMR). This is the measure of the energy used for routine functions such as breathing and cell repair — roughly 60 to 75 percent of the energy consumed by the body. During severe dieting, your BMR drops within 24 hours and can decline a full 20 percent within two weeks. This metabolic decline is one reason dieters often reach a steady unchanging period, and find that the same caloric intake which melted pounds earlier now produces no weight loss.

The body adapts to dieting in other ways. The enzyme lipoprotein lipase (脂肪酶), a chemical in the body, which controls how much fat is stored in fat cell, may become more active in some overweight people after they have lost weight. That would make the body more efficient at fat storage-exactly what the dieter doesn't want. And this change, like the drop in BMR, may be part of the reason dieters frequently regain their lost weight.

My interest in the yo-yo problem began in 1982, when my colleagues Thomas Wadden and Albert Stunkard and I were experimenting with very-low-calorie diets-800 calories or fewer per day. We hoped that patients in our clinic could lose large amounts of weight rapidly, then keep the weight loss with a behavior-modification program.

We found, however, that some people lost weight rapidly, some slowly; some lost for a while and then stopped losing. One woman, Marie, began the program at 230 pounds, reduced to 192 pounds, and then "hit a wall", even though she stayed on her diet and walked two miles a day. Marie, like many others in our program, had been a yo-yo dieter, and they tended to have the most difficulty in losing weight.

To see if such dieting could really change the body this way, other researchers and I began to study weight changes in animals. We fed a group of rats a high-fat diet until they became obese. Then we changed their diets repeatedly to make them lose weight, regain, lose again and regain again.

The results were surprising. The first time the rats lost weight, it took 21 days for them to go from obese to normal weight. On their second diet, it took 46 days, even though the rats consumed exactly as many calories.

With each yo-yo, it became easier for the rats to regain. After the first diet, they took 46 days to become obese again; after the second diet, they took only 14 days. In other words on the second yo-yo cycle, it took more than twice as long to lose-weight, and only one-third as long to regain it.

Surprised, our group contacted Harvard surgeon George Blackburn, a pioneer in the use of very-low-calorie diets. Blackburn and his colleagues reviewed the records of 140 dieters who had been through their weight-control clinic, had lost weight and regained it — and had returned for a second try. The records showed the dieters had lost an average of 2.3 pounds a week the first time, but only 1.3 pounds a week the second time.

Four years ago we began the Weight Cycling Project, a major study that includes some of the country's leading obesity researchers. We know that people who lose weight by dieting only and without an exercise program can lose a considerable amount of muscle. But then, if they gain weight back, they may regain less muscle and more fat. While the reason isn't clear, it may be easier for the body to put fat on than to rebuild lost muscle. We're asking if yo-yo dieters may lose fat from one part of the body and regain it elsewhere. For instance, according to our preparatory studies in animals, they could move fat to the abdomen. And research shows that abdominal fat raises the risk of heart disease and diabetes more than fat around the hips and thighs does.

None of this means that dieting is ineffective or foolish. For those who are 20 percent or more overweight, there are good reasons to reduce: successful weight loss can lower blood pressure and cholesterol, help control blood sugar in diabetics and enable people to feel better about themselves. But the new research does suggest that dieting must be taken seriously by people at any weight.

It also means that dieting alone is not the best way to weight control. When a weight-loss program includes exercise, you lose more fat and less muscle, and you're not likely to gain the weight back. That's because exercise may help resist the physiological changes that tend to come from yo-yo dieting.

Given the potential risks of yo-yo dieting, anyone who diets should be especially careful not to gain the weight back. Before you diet, ask yourself how determined you are; then set reasonable goals.

Permanent weight loss should be the main goal, so select a program that will help you change your life-style. Be careful of popular diet programs designed for rapid weight loss and filled with senseless tricks, such as going on and off a diet, eating "magic" foods and so on. A program should focus on sensible changes in nutrition and life-style. The best approach is a low-fat, high-complex-carbohydrate diet and regular physical exercise.

To avoid failing in the diet, recognize and plan for high-risk situations. If you always overeat when you visit your parents, for example, figure out how to get around that before your next visit. Understand that desires-for chocolate, say-are like waves that come up, will quickly subside. When the desire comes, get busy with a simple activity-reading or even brushing your teeth.

1. What is the risk that yo-yo dieting may bring according to the new research?

　A) It may damage the body's weight-control system seriously.

　B) It may make the task of losing weight more difficult.

　C) It may make it easier for the weight we lose to be regained.

　D) It may cause people fear for going on a diet.

2. What is the automatic reaction of your body when you are on diet?

A）It will consume more energy.

B）It will suffer from terrible heart break.

C）It will reduce your basal metabolic rate.

D）It will absorb more caloric intake automatically.

3. What is the basic function of enzyme lipoprotein lipase?

   A）To become active in order to lose weight.

   B）To control how much fat is stored in fat cell.

   C）To help cell regain the weight lost after being on diet.

   D）To drop the BMR of the dieter.

4. What does "hit a wall" mean when the author use it to refer Marie?

   A）It means that people achieved his goal of losing weight.

   B）It means that people stopped to stay on diet.

   C）It means that people started to walk two miles a day

   D）It means that people stepped into the most difficult stage of losing weight.

5. According to the author, the result of the rat research can be described as _____?

   A）disappointing B）exciting   C）meaningless D）surprising

6. What will happened on a dieter if he or she gain weight back without exercise?

   A）They may regain the same muscle and fat.

   B）They may regain more muscle and less fat.

   C）They may regain less muscle and more fat.

   D）They may become healthier than before

7. In order to lose weight permanently, which of the following advice that people should follow?

   A）Going on and off a diet.

   B）Eating magic foods.

   C）Avoiding being on diet.

   D）Eating low-fat, high-complex-carbohydrate diet and doing physical exercise regularly.

8. When a weight-loss program includes exercise, you lose more fat and less muscle, and you're not likely to _____.

9. In order to succeed in the diet one should know beforehand and make plans for _____.

10. When a dieter wants to eat chocolate, he or she should get busy with _____.

答案 1. A　2. B　3. C　4. D　5. D　6. C　7. D

8. gain the weight back　　9. high-risk situations

10. a simple activity, such as reading or brushing teeth

测评:

题　型 ＼ 正误题数	正确题数	错误题数
判断题		
选择题		
正确率		

备注: 正确率达80%以上为优秀, 70%以上为良好, 60%以上为合格

特训三及答案

New Proposals on Youth Employment

The unemployment rate in Japan continues to hover at around the 5% level, but the number of unemployed youths is exceptionally high compared to other age groups. The fluid situation is gradually taking root in society, with an increasing number of youths making a living as "freeters" (as young job-hoppers are called in Japan) or leaving and changing jobs even after they find employment. This youth employment problem is essentially a product of many companies' guarded stance (姿态) on employment and the narrowing of employment opportunities for those seeking to work as regular employees.

To deal with the youth employment problem, the government and relevant institutions have already presented various proposals for specific policies, such as to strengthen policies that can turn economic recovery into a vigorous increase of labor demand; while expanding job openings for regular employees, also to promote equal treatment of non-regular employees and secure opportunities for them to become regular employees so that the working styles of non-regular employees are not disadvantaged; from the earliest stage as possible, systematically to provide job preparatory education with a long-range outlook on career development. Some of these policies are actually being implemented, but they are not necessarily producing adequate results. For this reason, the following three new measures should be considered in addition to other measures being deliberated.

Reform of employment and recruitment practices

It is important that high school graduates are given as many opportunities as possible to select an occupation. While completely abolishing the one-person-one-company system on one hand, on the other hand, employment and career guidance should begin when students enter high school so they are well able to select an occupation on their own judgment.

Also, the year after graduation should be regarded as a period of joint follow-up by schools and employment agencies. Especially in regard to unemployed graduates and freeters, each party should assess the situation and support the employment of those young people.

With respect to college students, internship opportunities, career counseling, and other guidance schemes should be implemented soon after they enter college to eventually enable them to make independent career decisions.

Companies should give due consideration to the academic accomplishment of students when screening job applicants, as that is the primary function of students. Universities should draw upon France's baccalaureate system, for example, and introduce a system of university graduation examination or college academic certification test.

Finally, as a measure to expand employment opportunities, companies should amend their traditional practice of recruiting only prospective new graduates and open their doors to those who have already graduated.

Enhancing career education and the role of industries

Career education aiming to cultivate work values should be a consecutive (连续的) program provided over an ample amount of time beginning in the primary, junior high, and high school compulsory education stage.

In addition to teaching students about the significance of working and about occupations in general, career education should also include a course on "work and daily living" as a comprehensive course aiming to prepare students to become working members of society. The course should deal with a broad range of topics relating to the work concept, such as rights and obligations stipulated in labor laws, as well as with the mechanics of the pension system and other social security institutions and with such immediate issues as the environment and energy. Such a course would help youths to select their own lifestyles, including how to achieve a good balance between work and private life.

The industrial community should form organizations of companies (such as NPO) to address career education from a cross-cutting perspective and actively engage in activities to support the development of human resources for the next generation. For example, they are expected to develop and provide educational programs based on their unique technology and know-how, send personnel to schools, and offer funds and equipment.

In regional areas in Japan, activities to revitalize regional industries and promote new industries should be linked to model projects that incorporate regional characteristics and aim to foster and retain young people as future leaders of the region. For example, local governments could utilize the 500 or so young workers' centers throughout Japan as the bases of such projects with the cooperation of regional businesses and schools.

Proposal of a "career passport"

The "career passport" would function as a record of one's career and as a certification for the utilization of various support measures. It would be issued to all youths over the age of 18 and would be a passport to continuous support valid up to the age of 30 to 35.

The passport would contain a record of job changes, part-time experiences, studies, certifications and self-development efforts, in addition to accomplishments achieved through participation in volunteer and NPO activities. In this respect, it would take the form of an electronic card to allow the input and accumulation of information through a digital format that can be accessed by the individual whenever necessary.

The passport would enable young workers to receive career counseling regularly or as necessary at job cafes that are being newly established or at the more than 500 young worker's centers throughout Japan. They would also have the opportunity to check and evaluate their own careers, including part-time experiences, and effectively utilize various support programs for employment, capacity development and other areas necessary for developing their careers.

In addition to the above, a vocational scholarship system should be created to provide financial support for educational courses and school expenses to all young people who have graduated school — including the unemployed, freeters, and displaced workers — so that they may voluntarily prepare themselves for a job or develop their working capacities.

1. The youth frequent job changes result in many companies' guarded stance on their employment.

2. To offer different job opportunities to both youth regular and non-regular employees.

3. Employment and career guidance should be part of high school curriculum.

4. Companies should revise their policies to recruit both new and old graduates.

5. The school course should deal with a broad range of topics relating to the work concept such as job hunting and hopping.

6. There are about 500 youth centers in some local areas.

7. The career passport contains part-time experiences, studies, certificate and self-development except job-hopping.

8. College education should enable students to make _____.

9. Companies should provide educational program and send personnel to schools and offer _____.

10. In order to provide young people with financial support, we should create _____.

答案 1. Y 2. N 3. Y 4. Y 5. NG 6. N 7. N

8. their independence career decision

9. funds and equipment

10. a vocational scholarship system

特训四及答案

Our dreams combine verbal, visual and emotional stimuli into a sometimes broken, nonsensical but often entertaining story line. We can sometimes even solve problems in our sleep. Or can we? Many experts disagree on exactly what the purpose of our dreams might be.

Are they strictly random brain impulses, or are our brains actually working through issues from our daily life while we sleep — as a sort of coping mechanism? Should we even bother to interpret our dreams? Many say yes, that we have a great deal to learn from our dreams.

Why do we Dream?

For centuries, we've tried to figure out just why our brains play these nightly shows for us. Early civilizations thought dream worlds were real, physical worlds that they could enter only from their dream state. Researchers continue to toss around many theories about dreaming. Those theories essentially fall into two categories:

- The idea that dreams are only physiological stimulations
- The idea that dreams are psychologically necessary Physiological theories are based on the idea that we dream in order to exercise various neural connections that some researchers believe affect certain types of learning. Psychological theories are based on the idea that dreaming allows us to sort through problems, events of the day or things that are requiring a lot of our attention. Some of these theorists think dreams might be prophetic. Many researchers and scientists also believe that perhaps it is a combination of the two theories.

Dreaming and the BrainWhen we sleep, we go through five sleep stages. The first stage is a very light sleep from which it is easy to wake up. The second stage moves into a slightly deeper sleep, and stages three and four represent our deepest sleep. Our brain activity throughout these stages is gradually slowing down so that by deep sleep, we experience nothing but delta brain waves — the slowest brain waves. About 90 minutes after we go to sleep and after the fourth sleep stage, we begin REM sleep. Rapid eye movement (REM) was discovered in 1953 by University of Chicago researchers Eugene Aserinsky, a graduate student in physiology, and Nathaniel Kleitman, Ph. D. , chair of physiology. REM sleep is primarily characterized by movements of the eyes and is the fifth stage of sleep.

How to Improve Your Dream Recall

It is said that five minutes after the end of a dream, we have forgotten 50 percent of the dream's content. Ten minutes later, we've forgotten 90 percent of its content. Why is that? We don't forget our daily actions that quickly. The fact that they are so hard to remember makes their importance seem less. There are many resources both on the Web and in print that will give you tips on how to improve your recall of dreams. Those who believe we have a lot to learn about ourselves from our dreams are big proponents of dream journals. Here are some steps you can take to increase your dream recall:

- When you go to bed, tell yourself you will remember your dreams.
- Set your alarm to go off every hour and half so you'll wake up around the times that you leave REM sleep — when you're most likely to remember your dreams. (Or, drink a lot of water before you go to bed to ensure you have to wake up at least once in the middle of the night!)
- Keep a pad and pencil next to your bed.
- Try to wake up slowly to remain within the "mood" of your last dream.

Common Dream Themes and Their Interpretations

- Being naked in public

Most of us have had the dream at some point that we're at school, work or some social event, and we suddenly realize we forgot to put on clothes! Experts say this means:

◆ We're trying to hide something (and without clothes we have a hard time doing that).

◆ We're not prepared for something, like a presentation or test (and now everyone is going to know — we're exposed!). If we're naked but no one notices, then the interpretation is that whatever we're afraid of is unfounded. If we don't care that we're naked, the interpretation is that we're comfortable with who we are.

- Falling

You're falling, falling, falling… and then you wake up. This is a very common dream and is said to symbolize insecurities and anxiety. Something in your life is essentially out of control and there is nothing you can do to stop it. Another interpretation is that you have a sense of failure about something. Maybe you're not doing well in school or at work and are afraid you're going to be fired or expelled. Again, you feel that you can't control the situation.

- Being chased

The ever-popular chase dream can be extremely frightening. What it usually symbolizes is that you're running away from your problems. What that problem is depends on who is chasing you. It may be a problem at work, or it may be something about yourself that you know is destructive. For example, you may be drinking too much, and your dream may be telling you that your drinking is becoming a real problem.

- Taking an exam (or forgetting that you have one)

This is another very common dream. You suddenly realize you are supposed to be taking an exam at that very moment. You might be running through the hallways and can't find the classroom. This type of dream can have several variations that have similar meanings. (Maybe your pen won't write, so you can't finish writing your answers.) What experts say this may mean is that you're being scrutinized about something or feel you're being tested — maybe you're facing a challenge you don't think you're up to. You don't feel prepared or able to hold up to the scrutiny. It may also mean there is something you've neglected that you know needs your attention.

- Flying

Many flying dreams are the result of lucid dreaming (清醒梦). Not all flying dreams are, however. Typically, dreaming that you are flying means you are on top of things. You are in control of the things that matter to you. Or, maybe you've just gained a new perspective on things. It may also mean you are strong willed and feel like no one and nothing can defeat you. If you are having problems maintaining your flight, someone or something may be standing in the way of you having control. If you are afraid while flying, you may have challenges that you don't feel up to.

- Running, but going nowhere

This theme can also be part of the chasing dream. You're trying to run, but either your legs won't move or you simply aren't going anywhere — as if you were on a treadmill (踏车). According to some, this dream means you have too much on your plate. You're trying to do too many things at once and can't catch up or ever get ahead.

1. This passage mainly discusses different theories about why we have dreams at night.

2. Early theories held that dreams were reflection of people's real, physical worlds.

3. According to physiological theories, dreaming allows us to sort through problems or events of the day that require our attention.

4. REM occurs at the third and fourth stage during which we experience the deepest sleep.

5. The reason why dreams do not seem important is that they are very difficult to remember.

6. Trying to get recorded what you said or did in your dream can help increase your dream recall.

7. If a person dreams he is naked but is not noticed by others, it means what he is afraid of is groundless.

8. You're falling, falling, falling in your dream, which is said to symbolize _____.

9. Being chased in a dream usually means that you're escaping from your _____.

10. One of the interpretations for flying dreams is that you are and nothing _____ can defeat you.

答案　1. N　2. Y　3. N　4. N　5. Y　6. NG　7. Y

8. insecurities and anxiety

9. problems　10. strong willed

第二节　快速阅读模拟训练——拔高难度

特训一及答案

Will We Run Out of Water?

Picture a "ghost ship" sinking into the sand, left to rot on dry land by a receding sea. Then imagine dust storms sweeping up toxic pesticides and chemical fertilizers from the dry seabed and spewing them across towns and villages.

Seem like a scene from a movie about the end of the world? For people living near the Aral sea (咸海) in Central Asia, it's all too real. Thirty years ago, government planners diverted the rivers that flow into the sea in order to irrigate (provide water for) farmland. As a result, the sea has shrunk to half its original size, stranding (使搁浅) ships on dry land. The seawater has tripled in salt content and become polluted, killing all 24 native species of fish.

Similar large — scale efforts to redirect water in other parts of the world have also ended in ecological crisis, according to numerours environmenta groups. But many countries continue to build massive dams and irrigation systems, even though such projects can create more problems than they fix. Why? People in many parts of the world are desperate for water, and more people will need more water in the next century.

"Growing populations will worsen problems with water," says Peter H. Gleick, an environmental scientist at the Pacific Institute for studies in Development, Environment, and Security, a research organization in California. He fears that by the year 2025, as many as one — third of the world's projected (预测的) 8.3 billion people will suffer from water shortages.

Where water goes

Only 2.5 percent of all water on Earth is freshwater, water suitable for drinking and growing food, says Sandra Postel, director of the Global Water Policy Project in Amherst, Mass. Two — thirds of this freshwater is locked in glaciers (冰山) and ice caps (冰盖). In fact, only a tiny percentage of freshwater is part of the water cycle, in which water evaporates and rises into the atmosphere, then condenses and falls back to Earth as precipitation (rain or snow).

Some precipitation runs off land to lakes and oceans, and some becomes groundwater, water that seeps into the earth. Much of this renewable freshwater ends up in remote places like the Amazon river basin in Brazil, where few people live. In fact, the world's population has access to only 12,500 cubic kilometers of freshwater-about the amount of water in Lake Superior (苏必利尔湖). And people use half of this amount already. "If water demand continues to climb rapidly," says Postel, "there will be severe shortages and damage to the aquatic (水的) environment."

Close to home

Water woes (灾难) may seem remote to people living in rich countries like the United States. But Americans could face serious water shortages, too especially in areas that rely on groundwater. Groundwater accumulates in aquifers (地下蓄水层), layers of sand and gravel that lie between soil and bedrock. (For every liter of surface water, more than 90 liters are hidden underground.) Although the United States has large aquifers, farmers, ranchers, and cities are tapping many of them for water faster than nature can replenish (补充) it. In northwest Texas, for example, overpumping has shrunk groundwater supplies by 25 percent, according to Postel.

Americans may face even more urgent problems from pollution. Drinking water in the United States is generally safe and meets high standards. Nevertheless, one in five Americans every day unknowingly drinks tap water contaminated with bacteria and chemical wastes, according to the Environmental Protection Agency. In Milwaukee, 400,000 people fell ill in 1993 after drinking tap water tainted with cryptosporidium（隐孢子虫）, a microbe（微生物）that causes fever, diarrhea（腹泻）and vomiting.

The source

Where so contaminants come from? In developing countries, people dump raw（未经处理的）sewage（污水）into the same streams and rivers from which they draw water for drinking and cooking; about 250 million people a year get sick from water borne（饮水传染的）diseases.

In developed countries, manufacturers use 100,000 chemical compounds to make a wide range of products. Toxic chemicals pollute water when released untreated into rivers and lakes. (Certain compounds, such as polychlorinated biphenyls（多氯化联二苯）, or PCBs, have been banned in the United States.)

But almost everyone contributes to water pollution. People often pour household cleaners, car antifreeze, and paint thinners（稀释剂）down the drain; all of these contain hazardous chemicals. Scientists studying water in the San Francisco Bay reported in 1996 that 70 percent of the pollutants could be traced to household waste.

Farmers have been criticized for overusing herbicides and pesticides, chemicals that kill weeds and insects but insects but that pollute water as well. Farmers also use nitrates, nitrogen — rich fertilizer that helps plants grow but that can wreak havoc（大破坏）on the environment. Nitrates are swept away by surface runoff to lakes and seas. Too many nitrates "over-enrich" these bodies of water, encouraging the buildup of algae, or microscopic plants that live on the surface of the water. Algae deprive the water of oxygen that fish need to survive, at times choking off life in an entire body of water.

What's the solution?

Water expert Gleick advocates conservation and local solutions to water — related problems; governments, for instance, would be better off building small — scale dams rather than huge and disruptive projects like the one that ruined the Aral Sea.

"More than 1 billion people worldwide don't have access to basic clean drinking water," says Gleick. "There has to be a strong push on the part of everyone-governments and ordinary people-to make sure we have a resource so fundamental to life."

提示: 在实考试卷中, 8~10 题在答题卡 1 上。

1. That the huge water projects have diverted the rivers causes the Aral Sea to shrink.

2. The construction of massive dams and irrigation projects does more good than harm.

3. The chief causes of water shortage are population growth and water pollution.

4. The problems Americans face concerning water are ground water shrinkage and tap water pollution.

5. According to the passage all water pollutants come from household waste.

6. The people living in the United States will not be faced with water shortages.

7. Water expert Gleick has come up with the best solution to water-related problems.

8. According to Peter H. Gleick, by the year 2025, as many as _____ _____ of the world's people will suffer from water shortages.

9. Two-thirds of the freshwater on Earth is locked in _____.

10. In developed countries, before toxic chemicals are released into rivers and lakes, they should be treated in order to avoid _____.

答案 1. N 2. Y 3. N 4. N 5. Y 6. NG 7. Y

　　8. insecurities and anxiety 9. problems 10. strong willed

特训二及答案

Airplane Instruments

Modern airplanes are complicated machines. Pilots need many gauges（量表）and electronic aids to help fly them. The flight deck of a large passenger plane contains many indicator dials and warning lights. One of the most important instruments is the altimeter, which tells the pilot how high the plane is off the ground. The air speed indicator measures the plane's speed. The artificial horizon shows the position of the plane relative to the horizon. The turn and back indicator shows how much, if at all, the plane is turning and tilting. In dense clouds and fog, a pilot would not always know which way the plane is heading if it weren't for this instrument. A gyrocompass（旋转罗盘）and various radio devices are necessary for navigation.

Most large planes also have an automatic pilot. This is a device operated by a computer. It will fly the plane without the pilots touching the controls. These autopilots can even control takeoffs and landings. The flight deck also contains many gauges and meters that tell the pilot whether the many pieces of equipment on the plane are operating properly. They measure fuel level, temperatures, cabin pressure, electric current, etc. Indicators show whether the landing gear is up or down. The radio equipment allows the pilot to talk to ground controllers and to receive navigation signals.

Airplane Construction

Early airplanes were made of wood frames covered by fabric and held in shape by wire. After World War I, airplane designers started to use lightweight metals like aluminum, titanium, and magnesium alloys. A thin skin of metal was riveted into place over metal ribs. Strong epoxy（环氧的）glues are now used for some joints, instead of rivets. As planes grew in size, they became heavier. More powerful engines were developed in order to fly the heavier planes.

The use of metals brings with it a problem called metal fatigue. Stress and vibration in flight can cause metal parts eventually to break up. Airplanes must be constantly checked for signs of this trouble. Defective parts must be renewed by aircraft maintenance people.

Designers test scale models in wind tunnels before the full sized planes are built. Reactions of the models to high speed air streams give good indications how full sized planes will react in flight. This approach helps save a lot of money. It also helps to make airplanes safe.

Airport

An airport is a place where airplanes arrive and depart. Passengers leave and arrive on the airplanes and cargo is loaded and unloaded. Large, jet powered airplanes require long runways for takeoffs and landings. Big terminal buildings are necessary to handle thousands of passengers and their baggage. Very large airports usually serve several large cities and cover thousands of acres. Hundreds of planes arrive and depart daily. All this traffic must be carefully controlled to avoid delays and accidents. This is done from a control tower. The tower stands high above the ground. Air traffic controllers, inside the tower, must be able to guide airplanes through their takeoffs and landings.

Large airports are often like small cities. Many have post offices, banks, hotels, restaurants, and many kinds of shops. Airports have their own fire and police departments, fuel storage tanks, and repair work shops. Some companies even have their shipping warehouses located at airports.

One of the largest airports in the world is in Grapevine, Texas, midway between the cities of Dallas and Fort Worth. This airport covers 7 200 hectares (18,000 acres). Its five terminals can handle the arrivals and departures of 90 jumbo jets at the same time. O'Hare International Airport, in Chicago, is the busiest airport in the world. It handles more than 37 million passengers a year.

Small airports that are used only by private airplanes usually cover 20 to 40 hectares (50 to 100 acres). They do not need all the buildings and services of a large airport. The control tower may be just a small room in a building at ground level.

Runways

Early planes were light. Early runways were sometimes just level grass fields. Paved runways became necessary when airplanes became heavier and faster. Today's big jet planes weigh hundreds of tons. They move along runways at speeds of 160 kph (100 mph). When they land, the runways take a lot of pounding and must be made of concrete or asphalt (沥青). They must have solid foundations and a surface that prevents skidding.

Airplanes take off into the wind in order to get better lift. They also land into the wind to have better control as they slow down. Most airports have runways pointing in different directions. This means that there are always runways on which airplanes can go into the wind as they take off and land.

Heavily loaded passenger jets need long runways to gather enough speed to leave the ground. Runways at some large airports are longer than 3,000m (10,000 ft).

At night, bright lights line the runways so that pilots can find them without trouble. A system of flashing guide lights is set up beyond the runway to help pilots land safely.

Control Towers

People who work in control towers are called air traffic controllers. They direct the movements of all planes on the ground and in the air by keeping track of them on large radar screens. Air traffic controllers tell a pilot, by radio, when and where to taxi or pilot the plane down the runway.

Electronic equipment is used to guide airplanes. Long range radar is used to keep track of planes far away from the airport. This radar is called Ground Control Approach (GCA). When the airplane gets within a few miles of the runway, the air traffic controller begins to use Precision Approach Radar (PAR). This allows the controller to guide the airplane to within 0.4km (0.25mi) of the runway. At that point, the pilot completes the landing. Another electronic aid used in bad weather is the Instrument Landing System (ILS). In this system, radio transmitters located near the runway send guidance signals to the airplane. These signals tell the pilot how to steer the plane for the final approach to the runways. Today, there are also electronic "microwave" landing systems (MLS) that can land the plane fully automatically.

Terminal Buildings

Terminal buildings vary in size and shape. Most of them are quite large. More than 228 million people fly on the airlines in America every year. Every passenger must pass through terminals. Long, covered walkways lead from the center of some terminals to the gates where airplanes are boarded. At some airports, buses are used to transport passengers to their airplanes. Passengers arriving from another country must pass through customs and passport control. Customs officials check the incoming baggage for taxable items. They also check passengers to be sure no forbidden items are brought into the country. Passport officials check the passports of passengers for personal identification.

Passengers are not allowed to bring guns, knives, or other weapons onto a passenger airplane. Before boarding, they must walk through a detector which triggers a special signal if they are carrying anything made of metal. Luggage is also examined for weapons. This is done to ensure the safety of the passengers.

1. The main purpose of this passage is to introduce the history of airplanes.

2. The device of an automatic pilot can usually fly a plane more smoothly than a human pilot.

3. With the help of the radio equipment, pilots are able to communicate with ground controllers.

4. We can tell from the passage that early airplanes are not as solid as modern ones.

5. According to the passage, the busiest airport in the world is in Grapevine, Texas, midway between the cities of Dallas and Fort Worth.

6. The runways should be long and solid enough for the heavily loaded jets.

7. Precision Approach Radar (PAR) is used by air traffic controllers to keep track of airplanes far away from the airport.

8. The planes can be landed fully automatically if the control towers are equipped with _____.

9. After getting off the plane, every passenger arriving from another country must pass through _____.

10. When passengers go through a detector before they board, and anything made of metal is detected, the detector triggers _____.

答案 1. N 2. NG 3. Y 4. Y 5. N 6. Y 7. N

8. electronic "microwave" landing systems

9. customs and passport control

10. a special signal

特训三及答案

Six Ways to Remove Stress at the Dinner Table

What is your dinnertime like? Maybe "dinner" consists of cold takeaway food, eaten alone in front of the TV while you surf the Internet and answer e-mail, or perhaps the eat-and-run dinners you share with your spouse or partner barely leave you time to say "hello" and "goodbye" to each other. Or maybe your kitchen is starting to resemble a fast-food restaurant, with family members coming in and out and grabbling a bite between activities.

While the dinner hour once represented a calm shelter from the day's storm, today it is often anything but relaxing.

"We're hurried; we've turned up the volume of our lives to such a high number that we often can't even see how stressed we are. And we almost never see how we bring that stress to the dinner table, a place where traditionally we sought relaxation and comfort," says Mini Donaldson, a stress and time management expert.

Recent research at Columbia University found that children who regularly had dinner with their families are less likely to abuse drugs or alcohol, and more likely to do better in school. In fact, studies show the best-adjusted children are those who eat with an adult at least five times a week. Many studies support the importance of family mealtime in decreasing the incidence of teens who smoke, drink alcohol, participate in sex at a young age, start flights, get suspended from school, or commit suicide.

And kids aren't the only ones who benefit from a peaceful mealtime. Couples are well as singles benefit when mealtime is a relaxing experience.

It is not only better for the soul and spirit to dine quietly and slowly — even if you are alone — but it is also good for the digestion. Of course, knowing we should relax at dinner time is one thing; actually doing it is something else. To help you get started, six guidelines for creating a mealtime experiences which everyone will look forward to are as follows.

1. Turn down the volume.

Nothing brings down the stress level like turning down the volume of your environment.

That mean no cell phone, no TV, and no radios blaring in the background, and it means not answering the phone during mealtime.

Let each family member contribute suggestions about what to play, or let a different person pick the soft background music for each meal. A good family project is creating an hour music that includes everyone's favorite relaxing tunes,

2. Set the table to set the mood.

While you may not want to pull out the good china for every meal, a brightly colored tablecloth is simple way to give a special look and feel even to your old kitchen plates. It is best to make any table setting seem more relaxing, even when the plates don't match. In addition, buy an inexpensive bouquet of fresh flowers for the table. It doesn't have to be decline, but it sends the message that dinner is special and we are special, too.

3. Let there be (soft) light.

Dimming the lighting in the room and adding some candles on the dinner table can go a long way in lowering everyone's stress level.

Candles also traditionally make an occasion, so lighting them at dinner table is a way of "This meal is special — we are special." If you have young children, try using one large candle set in a weighted base to ensure it doesn't matter fall over. You can also turn lighting the candle into part of the dinner ritual-something that signals the start of a meal — and let a different child do the lighting each time.

4. Control the conversation

Too often we see dinner with our partner or family as an opportunity for family as an opportunity for complaint. This can be particularly true for parents, who may turn the dinner hour into a discipline hour, often because they feel it's the only time they have their child's attention.

To avoid this, you can establish a few ground rules for dinner time conversation. Be positive and postpone negative comments for another time. Avoid lecturing and scolding, and instead reward good manners and good behavior with positive comments.

Furthermore, don't use mealtime to discuss the "honey-do" list, your medical problem, or why you hate your boss, or your mother. Instead, prompt engaging conversation by discussing the highlights of your day, or by planning a fantasy vacation — discussing where you'd go if you could go anywhere in the world.

Make it a time that centers on the positive things that happened that week or that day. It's the time to tell your spouse or your children, or both, that what they did that week or that day made you really proud.

5. Keep cool in the kitchen.

The table can look great, the music may be delightful, the food might smell terrific, but if the cook is irritated, those at the table will be irritated as well.

When you get home, take a few minutes before heading into the kitchen. Take a deep breath, and whether you have 30 minutes, try to put the day behind you. It helps to get as many dinner-related tasks done ahead of time as you can. Wash the vegetables for salads the night before. The less you have to do at mealtime, the more relaxed you will be and the more relaxed your family will feel.

6. Keep it real.

While it would be great if you could make every meal a shelter from a storm, realistically, there are days when that are just not going to happen.

Family meals do not have to take place every night, nor do they need extensively planning. To make relaxing meals a reality, schedule them on your calendar, And remember, that dinner isn't the only time you can have a special meal. If breakfast is easier to plan than a dinner meal, make a commitment to gather in the morning several time a week.

It's the sharing and bonding — not the food — that matter most.

1. People's now have dinner with their families in _____ manner.

　　A) relaxed　　B) hurried　　C) leisured　　D) polite

2. According to the author, why dinner is no longer comfortable now?

　　A) Because it barely has any nutrition.

　　B) Because the wife's cooking is bad.

　　C) Because people like eating hurriedly.

　　D) Because people usually bring stress to the dinner table.

3. In the first three paragraphs, which one is not mentioned?

　　A) Many people don't want to have dinner with their families.

　　B) Many people would like to buy takeaway food.

   C) Many people have the habit of having dinner while surfing the Internet.

   D) Now the dinner hour is often anything but relaxing.

4. If the parents often join the children for the dinner, the children will.

   A) Smoke and drink alcohol.

   B) Fight with others or commit suicide.

   C) Perform bad in school.

   D) Be less likely to abuse drugs or alcohol.

5. When having family dinner, what kind of volume background is favorite?

   A) Listening to the radio.

   B) Answering the phone during mealtime.

   C) Picking the soft background music for the senior.

   D) Playing various soft tunes favored by everybody.

6. According to the passage, why lighting candles is suggested during dinner time?

   A) The families will feel they are valued.

   B) The families don't like strong light.

   C) Soft light makes a romantic atmosphere.

   D) The electricity is sometimes cut off.

7. When having a dinner conversation, _____ should be mentioned.

   A) complaint

   B) discipline

   C) positive comments

   D) why you hate your boss

8. Dinner time can be cheerful and relaxing when people take about positive things instead of _____.

9. Dinners can't be wonderful unless the cook frees himself or herself _____.

10. What is more important to the family members is not the food itself but _____.

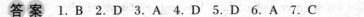

答案　1. B　2. D　3. A　4. D　5. D　6. A　7. C

8. making negative comments
9. from irritation
10. the sharing and the bonding

特训四及答案

We often focus on building relationships with others that we forget the essential first step: being friends of ourselves. That is the crucial first step if we are to have good relationships with others. How can we have good relationships with others if we don't even have good relationship with ourselves? The problem might be worse than we expect. Maybe we don't like ourselves without realizing it. Here is a simple checklist: is there anything you don't like about yourself from these lists?

Your past

Maybe you have made mistakes in the past which you feel bad about. You might be disappointed with yourself on why you could make such mistakes. Even if that happened in distant past, your subconscious mind still has a reason not to like yourself.

Your background

You might wish that you were born in different family, or that you have different background. Maybe you could not accept the fact that you are not as lucky as others, who seem to get whatever they want effortlessly because of their background.

Your personality traits

You might have some personality traits that you don't like. For example, you may be an introvert and you don't like it; you wish you are an extrovert.

Your achievements relative to others, others might have better achievements than you, and no matter how hard you tried, it might seem impossible for you to match them. You might then think that it's because you are not smart enough or don't have enough talents. Is there anything that resonates with you? All these give reasons to you not to like yourself. That in turn makes it difficult for you to be a good friend to yourself.

Fortunately, there are always things you can do to fix the situation. Here are some tips:

1. Forgive yourself.

You may have made those mistakes in the past, but is there anything you can do about them? I don't think so, except learning from them. It's true that you are not perfect, but neither is everybody else. It's normal to make mistakes, so do yourself a favor by giving yourself forgiveness.

2. Accept things you can't change.

There are some things you cannot change, such as your background and your past. So learn to accept them. You will feel much relieved if you treat things you can't change the way they deserve: just accept them, smile, and move on.

3. Focus on your strengths.

Instead of focusing on your weaknesses, focus on your strengths. You always have some strength which give you a unique combination nobody else have. Recognize your strengths and build your life around them.

4. Write your success stories.

One reason we may not like ourselves is we are too focused on what we don't have that we forget about what we have. So make a list of your achievements; write your success stories. They do not have to be big things; there are a lot of small but important achievements in our life. For example, if you have some good friends, that's already an achievement. If you have a good family, that is also an achievement.

5. Stop comparing yourself with others.

You are unique. You can never be like other people, and neither can other people be like you. The way you measure your success is not determined by other people and what they achieve. Instead, it is determined by your own life purpose. You have everything you need to achieve your life purpose, so it's useless to compare yourself with others.

6. Always be true to yourself

You don't like other people lying to you, right? Similarly, you won't like yourself if you know that you lie to yourself. Whether you realize it or not, that gives your mind a reason not to like yourself. That's why it's important to always be true to yourself. In whatever you do, be honest and follow your conscience. Remember this quote by Abraham Lincoln:

I desire so to conduct the affairs of this administration that if at the end... I have lost every other friend on earth, I shall at least have one friend left, and that friend shall be down inside of me.

1. Which one is Not mentioned about something you don't like yourself?

    A) People's past.   B) People's background.
    C) People's character.   D) People's habits.

2. According the article, how many trips you can do to change the situation of being a friend to yourself.

    A) 4   B) 5   C) 6   D) 7

3. When you feel others achievements are better than you, and it is hard for you to match them. Firstly, you should think that _____.

    A) everyone has mistakes everyday

    B) write a success story

    C) giving myself forgiveness

    D) I have a lot of things to improve

4. In the sixth part, what does the author want to tell _____.

    A) what your achievement depends on

    B) how to make a friend to yourself

    C) why we cannot match others

    D) the reasons why it is difficult for us to make a friend to yourself

5. There are many small but important things for us to _____.

A) write success stories

B) share with our friends

C) encourage ourselves in our life

D) talk to others

6. The way you measure your success is _____.

A) determined by other people

B) determined by what we achieved

C) determined by our character

D) determined by our life purpose

7. The author's attitude towards this article is _____.

A) negative   B) positive

C) indifferent   D) not mentioned

8. If we are to have good relationships with others, the important first step is _____.

9. We should pay more attention to _____ rather than weakness.

10. One reason we may not like ourselves is _____.

答案　1. D　2. C　3. C　4. D　5. A　6. D　7. B

8. being friends of ourselves

9. our strengths

10. we are too focused on what we don't have that we forget about what we have

第三节　篇章词汇阅读与简答模拟训练——应试难度

特训一及答案

    As the pace of life continues to increase, we are fast losing the art of relaxation. But relaxation is __1__ for a healthy mind and body.

    Stress is a natural part of everyday life and there is no way to __2__ it. In fact, it is not the bad thing as it is often supposed to be. A certain amount of stress is vital to provide motivation and give purpose to life. It is only when the stress gets out of ___3___ that it can lead to poor performance and ill health.

The amount of stress a person can withstand depends very much on the individual. Some peoplw are not afraid of stress, and such ___4___ are obviously prime material for managerial responsibilities. Others lose heart at the first sight of ___5___ difficulties. When exposed to stress, in whatever form, we react both physically and ___6___. In fact we make choice between "flight or fight" and in more ___7___ days the choices made the difference between life or death. The crises we meet today are unlikely to be so extreme, but however little the stress, it involves the same ___8___. It is when such a reaction lasts long, through continued ___9___ to stress, that health becomes endangered. Since we cannot ___10___ stress from our lives it would be unwise to do so even if we could, we need to find ways to deal with it.

A) exposure　　B) characters　　C) answer　　D) chemically
E) avoid　　F) psychologically　　G) primitive　　H) transfer
I) unusual　　J) control　　K) remove　　L) escape
M) response　　N) backward　　O) essential

答案

解析:

1. 选 O)。此处应填形容词。前文中说人们正在失去放松的休闲方式，But 转折表明作者对 relaxation 的重视态度，只有 essential "必须的，重要的"符合文意。

2. 选 E)。此处应填动词。前句说 Stress is a natural part of everyday life "压力是日常生活中很自然的一部分"，说明人们不能避免压力。选项中只有 avoid 的意思为"避免，消除"，故选 E) avoid 正确。

3. 选 J)。此处应填名词。前面说有压力并不是坏事，适当的压力能给人以动力，能赋予人生活的意义。只有在……时候，压力才会导致人们表现不佳，身体不好。根据上下文可知 get out of control "压力失控" 的时候，才会有不好的结果，故选 J) control。

4. 选 B)。此处应填名词。前句中 not afraid of stress "不怕压力" 是一些人的性格特点，选项中可以表示人的性格特点的词只有 characters，故选 B)。

5. 选 I)。此处应填形容词，修饰名词 difficulties。一些人遇到……的困难就灰心丧气，选项中的形容词中，unusual "不同寻常的" 可以说明困难的程度，故选择 I)。

6. 选 F)。此处应填副词，与 physically 相对应，在此 physically 作为 "身体上的" 解释。选项中的副词有 chemically "化学地" 和 psychologically "精神地"，很明显两个副词中选择 F) psychologically。

7. 选 G)。此处应填形容词，修饰名词 days。days 与后文中的 today 相对应，形成对比。选项中的是 primitive，即将人类的早期和人类的今天做比较，故选 G)。而 N) backward 说明的是社会发展的状态，不符合原文意思。

8. 选 M)。此处填名词。前句说，在人类的早期，选择不同就意味着生与死的差别；而现在人们碰到的危机不可能那样极端。后面 but 转折，说明了不管是压力的大小，人们都是在 "避免" 和 "战斗" 之间选择，下句中的 such a reaction 也可以说明人们对压力的反应是一样的，选项中的名词 answer 和 response 中，M) response = reaction 符合文意。

9. 选 A)。根据上题，这种反应长时间持续的原因就是长时间的面对压力，选项中的 exposure "暴露的状态，受影响" 符合上下文意思，故选择 A) exposure。

10. 选 K)。此处要填动词原形，和 from 构成动介搭配。人们应想办法应对压力，而不是将它……出人们的生活。选项中的 transfer 表示 "转移" 不符合原文意思；remove "移动，移除" 可以和 from 连用，表示 "除掉，移开"，符合原文意思，故选 K)。

特训二及答案

Try out

We call it the "common cold" for good reason. There are over one billion colds in the United States each year. You and your children will probably have more colds than any other type of __1__. Children average three to eight colds per year. They continue getting them __2__ childhood. Parents often get them from the kids. Colds are the most common reason that children __3__ school and parents miss work.

Children usually get colds from other children. When a new __4__ is introduced into a school or day __5__, it quickly travels through the class.

Colds can __6__ year-round, but they occur mostly in the winter (even in areas with mild winters). In areas where there is no winter, colds are most __7__ during the rainy season.

When someone has a cold, his runny nose is teeming with (充满) cold __8__. Sneezing, nose-blowing, and nose-wiping spread the virus. You can __9__ a cold by inhaling the virus if you are sitting close to someone who sneezes, or by __10__ your nose, eyes, or mouth after you have touched something contaminated (污染的) by the virus.

People are most contagious (会感染的) for the first 2 to 3 days of a cold, and usually not contagious at all by day 7 to 10.

A) care   I) catch   B) throughout   J) moving
C) touching   K) strain   D) occur   L) illness
E) abuse   M) miss   F) sensation   N) common
G) tension   O) by   H) viruses

答案

解析：

1. 选 L）。此处需要一个名词。感冒也是一种病，这里指的是你和你的小孩患感冒的几率比其他任何一种病的几率都大，故选 illness。

2. 选 B）。此处需要一个介词。因为所接的词"childhood"是一个时间段概念，在这个持续性的时间里，感冒也经常发生。

3. 选 M）。此处需要一个动词。感冒是导致学生不能正常上学的普遍原因，"miss school"表示耽误学业。

4. 选 K）。此处需要一个名词。"strain"的意思之一为"（疾病的）类型"，而备选答案中的"tension"只表示"紧张，不安"。

5. 选 A）。此处需要一个名词。"day care"意思为（托儿所的）日托，正好符合上下文的意思。

6. 选 D）。此处需要一个动词。"occur"表示"出现，发生"，而且后文说在冬天，感冒的情况出现得更加频繁，进一步确定了答案应该是"occur"。

7. 选 N）。此处需要一个形容词。在没有冬季的地区，雨季是感冒的高发期。

8. 选 H）。此处需要一个名词。当一个人患感冒时，他不停流鼻涕的鼻子中肯定充满了病毒。

9. 选 I）。此处需要一个动词。"catch a cold"是固定搭配，表示患感冒。

10. 选 C）。此处需要一个动名词。当你触摸过带有病毒的东西，再触摸自己的鼻子、眼睛或嘴，就会被感染，所以选 touching 再合适不过了。

特训三及答案

Many American students ___1___ higher education to prepare for professional employment. In your academic training you will need to begin planning for the ___2___ from college to career. A career is really a process-it is how you progress through a ___3___ of jobs and occupations during your working years. A college education can help you get started on your career journey.

In America society, the type of occupational fields you choose and jobs you hold ___4___ your entire lifestyle: yourself concept, income, prestige, choice of friends, and where you will live. This freedom to choose from thousands of employment choices can be ___5___ or troubling-if you don't know where and how to begin.

　　Career planning is a comprehensive process that takes much time and ___6___ . Career planning can greatly increase your ___7___ of obtaining employment in the occupation you choose. However, career planning includes much more than a job search. It begins with carefully considering what you want and need in life.

　　Career planning can be divided into four ___8___ steps that include self-assessment, occupational exploration and selection, career preparation, and job seeking. Although each student's goal will be ___9___ , one suggested timetable to help you keep on course is to complete one step in each university year. Your ___10___ may be longer or shorter depending on your career goal.

A) transmission 　　I) superficial 　　B) consecutive

J) effort 　　C) enjoyable 　　K) prospects

D) series 　　L) influence 　　E) perspective

F) varies 　　M) cultivate 　　G) schedule

N) pursue 　　H) different 　　O) transition

答 案

解析：

1. 选N）。答案应该是个动词，因此F），M），N），L）可能当选。根据空格前的students，可以排除F）varies. 结合试题句意，答案为N）pursue（追求）。

2. 选O）。答案应该是个名词。如果可以看懂试题所在的句子，就可以选对O），本题考查重点是transmission（播送，传染）和transition（过渡），如果不能区分这两个词的词义，就有可能选错。

3. 选D）。a series of 表示"一系列"为固定搭配。

4. 选L）。答案应该是个动词。选项F）可以被轻易排除。

5. 选 C）。答案应该是个形容词，根据后面的："or troubling"来判断，enjoyable 是它的反义词，另一个形容词 consecutive，可能会产生干扰，但 troubling 已经决定了只有 enjoyable 正确。

6. 选 J）。根据文章的意思，"职业规划是很花费时间和努力的。"

7. 选 K）。K）答案应该是个名词，根据句意，选项 K）prospects 单词认知有难度，同时 E）perspective 也具有极大的干扰性，本题难度最大。

8. 选 B）。根据句子结构，答案应该是个形容词。

9. 选 H）。答案应该为形容词，将备选单词带入原句，答案不难。

10. 选 G）。答案应该是个名词，只剩下 G）schedule 了。

特训四及答案

The main energy foods are the carbohydrates （碳水化合物）. These are sugars and starch（淀粉）. Wheat and rice are rich in starch and fruits and vegetables contain __1__ amount of sugar, honey and jam are also rich in sugar.

Like carbohydrates fats are food that provides energy. Butter, certain types of fish, eggs are rich in fats. Fats can be stored in various parts of the body as __2__ of energy. Because fats in general are slowly __3__, they satisfy hunger for long periods.

Proteins （蛋白质）are very complex __4__. The body needs proteins for the growth of new cells and for the repair and __5__ of old cells. Foods rich in proteins are __6__ to a balanced diet. Milk, some vegetables, meat, chicken, fish, cheese are some foods rich in proteins.

A good diet will certain a __7__ of foods so that the body contains all the minerals It needs for good health.

Vitamins are necessary for the __8__ working of the body. Water __9__ up about 70 percent of the weight of the human body. The average adult needs about two liters of water daily to replace the water the body __10__.

A）loosen　　　　I）induced　　　　B）variety

J）identical　　　C）makes　　　　K）reserves

D）proper　　　　L）digested　　　E）loses

M）considerable　F）preserves　　N）diversity

G）essential　　　O）replacement　H）substances

答案

解析：

1. 选 M）。答案应该是个形容词，根据空格后的 amount 可以判断，considerable 相当多的相当大的。

2. 选 K）。根据句意，空白处应该是一个名词。从 of energy 可以判断出，脂肪是能量的储存物。

3. 选 L）。整句话的意思是要表达"脂肪一般在身体里消化的很慢，是因为它们能在一段长的时间能控制住人饿"。

4. 选 H）。这句话的含义是说"蛋白质是一个很复杂的……."，根据所填之处在整个句子的中是扮演名字的角色。根据选项，只有 H）符合，为"物质"的意思。

5. 选 O）。从前后句子中的"new cells"和后面的"old cells"，可以判断出，此处为"replacement"为"替换"的含义。

6. 选 G）。答案应该是个形容词，根据空格后的 to，再结合句意，在理应选 G）。

7. 选 B）。本题考查的是固定搭配：a variety of 的用法，为"多种的，多样的"。

8. 选 D）。空白处应该是一个形容词，根据句子的含义：维他命对身体适当的工作是很有必要的。

9. 选 C）。本题同样考查的是固定搭配 make up 的用法，在这里的意思是：组成，构成。

10. 选 E）。答案应是个动词，根据空格前的 replace the water 可以判断。

第四节 篇章词汇阅读与简答模拟训练——拔高难度

特训一及答案

There's no question that the Earth is getting hotter. The real questions are: How much of the warming is our fault, and are we __1__ to slow the devastation by controlling our insatiable __2__ for fossil fuels?

Global warming can seem too __3__ to worry about, or too uncertain — something projected by the same computer __4__ that often can't get next week's weather right. On a raw winter day you might think that a few degrees of warming wouldn't be such a bad thing anyway. And no doubt about it: Warnings about __5__ change can sound like an environmentalist scare tactic, meant to force us out of our cars and restrict our lifestyles.

Comforting thoughts, perhaps. Unfortunately, however, the Earth has some discomforting news.

From Alaska to the snowy peaks of the Andes the world is heating up right now, and fast. Globally, the __6__ is up 1°F over the past century, but some of the coldest, most remote spots have warmed much more. The results aren't pretty. Ice is __7__, rivers are running dry, and coasts are __8__, threatening communities.

The __9__ are happening largely out of sight. But they shouldn't be out of mind, because they are omens of what's in store for the __10__ of the planet.

A) remote   B) techniques   C) consisting   D) rest
E) Willing   F) climate   G) skill   H) appetite
I) melting   J) vanishing   K) eroding   L) temperature
M) curiosity   N) changes   O) skillful

答 案

解析:

1. 选 E)。此处应填入 E) 项,be willing to 为固定搭配。

2. 选 H)。此处应填入一个名词,而 appetite 通常和介词 for 搭配,此处句子的意思为控制我们无止境的欲望。

3. 选 A)。此处应填入一个形容词,根据上下文意思应选 A) 项,意为:全球气候变暖似乎离我们太遥远,以至于我们无需为此担心。

4. 选 B)。此处应填入一个名词,而与 computer 搭配的名词在选项中根据上下文意思 B) 为正确选项。

5. 选 F)。根据上下文意思此处应表达气候变化之意,因此 F) 为正确选项。

6. 选 L)。该题较为简单,表示"上个世纪全球的气温上升了 1 华氏度",应能迅速找出正确答案。

7. 选 I)。显然 ice 与 melt 搭配,因此 I) 为正确选项。

8. 选 K)。此处应填入一个现在分词,表示"海岸受到侵蚀",因此应选 K。

9. 选 N)。该题较为简单,应填入一个复数名词,所以填入 N) 项。

10. 选 D)。the rest of 为固定搭配。

特训二及答案

As the plane circled over the airport, everyone sensed that something was wrong. The plane was moving unsteadily through the air, and ___1___ the passengers had fastened their seat belts, they were suddenly ___2___ forward. At that moment, the air-hostess ___3___. She looked very pale, but was quite ___4___. Speaking quickly but almost in a whisper, she ___5___ everyone that the pilot had ___6___ and asked if any of the passengers knew anything about machines or at ___7___ how to drive a car. After a moment ___8___, a man got up and followed the hostess into the pilot's cabin. Moving the pilot ___9___, the man took his seat and listened carefully to the ___10___ instructions that were being sent by radio from the airport below. The plane was now dangerously close to ground, but to everyone's relief, it soon began to climb.

A) although   B) anxious   C) thrown   D) shifted
E) appeared   F) urgent   G) presented   H) aside
I) even   J) informed   K) calm   L) least
M) fainted   N) length   O) hesitation

答 案

解析：

1. 选 A）。本句意为尽管乘客们都已经系好安全带，他们还是被突然向前抛去。although "尽管"，引导让步状语从句，符合句意。
2. 选 C）。根据上题注释，shift "转移"，这里选择 throw "扔、抛"，最为合适。
3. 选 E）。present 呈现、陈述，及物动词；appear 出现，符合句意。
4. 选 K）。well "健康的"；still "静止的"；calm "镇静的"；quiet "安静的"。前句说她看上去脸色苍白，后半句进行转折，calm 最符合句意。
5. 选 J）。inform "通知、告诉"，符合句意。
6. 选 M）。faint "昏迷、晕倒"，最符合句意。
7. 选 L）。at least "至少"；at length "详细地"。at least 最符合句意。
8. 选 O）。hesitation "犹豫"。hesitation 最符合句意。
9. 选 H）。本句意为把飞行员挪到一边。aside 意为 "一边、旁边"，符合句意。
10. 选 F）。本句意为这个人坐到飞行员的座位上，认真听发自下面机场通过无线电发出的紧急指令。anxious "焦急的" 不符合句意。只有 urgent 合适。

特训三及答案

The most exciting kind of education is also the most personal.

Nothing can exceed the joy of discovering for yourself something that is important to you! It may be an idea or a bit of information you come across accidentally, or a sudden insight, fitting together pieces of information or working through a problem. Such personal encounters are the "payoff" in education. A teacher may direct you to learning and even encourage you in it-but no teacher can make the excitement or the joy happen. That's up to you.

A research paper, assigned in a course and perhaps checked at various stages by an instructor, leads you beyond classrooms, beyond the texts for classes and into a process where the joy of discovery and learning can come to you many times. Preparing the research paper is an active and individual process, and ideal learning process. It provides a structure within which you can make exciting discoveries, of knowledge and of self, that are basic to education. But the research paper also gives you a chance to individualize a school assignment, to suit a piece of work to your own interests and abilities, to show others what you can do. Writing a research paper is more than just a classroom exercise. It is an experience in searching out, understanding and synthesizing, which forms the basis of many skills applicable to both academic and nonacademic tasks. It is, in the fullest sense, a discovering, an education. So, to produce a good research paper is both a useful and a thoroughly satisfying experience!

To some, the thought of having to write an assigned number of pages, often more than ever produced before, is disconcerting. To others, the very idea of having to work independently is threatening. But there is no need to approach the research paper assignment with anxiety, and nobody should view the research paper as an obstacle to overcome. Instead, consider it a goal to accomplish, a goal within reach if you use the help this book can give you.

1. What does the writer mean by "Such personal encounters are the 'payoff' in education" (Line 4, Para. 1)?

2. It can be inferred from the passage that writing a research paper gives one chances to _____.

3. According to the second paragraph, writing a research paper is not only a classroom exercise, it is also _____.

4. The writer argues in the passage that one should consider research paper writing _____.

5. What will probably follow this passage?

答 案

1. He means that it is through education that we can have such personal encounters as discovering a sudden insight.

2. fully develop one's personal abilities

3. an experience, a discovering, an education

4. a pleasure, not a burden

5. How to write a research paper.

特训四及答案

In recent years, more and more foreigners are involved in the teaching programs of the United States. Both the advantages and the disadvantages ____1____ using foreign faculty in teaching positions have to be ____2____, of course. It can be said that the foreign background that makes the faculty member from abroad an asset also ____3____ problems of adjustment, both for the university and for the individual. The foreign research scholar usually isolates himself in the laboratory as a means of protection; ____4____, what he needs is to be fitted to a highly organized university system quite different from ____5____ at home. He is faced in his daily work with differences in philosophy, arrangements of courses and methods of teaching. Both the visiting professor and his students ____6____ a common ground in each other's cultures, some concept of what is already in the minds of American students is ____7____ for the foreign professor.

While helping him to adapt himself to his new environment, the university must also ___8___ certain adjustments in order to take full advantage of what the newcomer can ___9___. It isn't always known how to make creative use of foreign faculty, especially at smaller colleges. This is thought to be a ___10___ where further study is called for. The findings of such a study will be of value to colleges and universities with foreign faculty.

A) field	B) possess	C) considered	D) express
E) offer	F) create	G) required	H) of
I) emerge	J) make	K) lack	L) however
M) scope	N) cause	O) that	

答 案

解析:

1. 选 H) 使用外国教师的优点和缺点必须仔细权衡, 此处空格填介词 of。

2. 选 C) consider 意思是"考虑, 认为"。使用外国教师的优点和缺点必须仔细权衡, 此处用被动态。

3. 选 F) create 意思是"产生, 制造"。国外的教师资源也会产生些问题。

4. 选 L) 本句与前一句意思为转折关系, 而且转折词在前, 因此用连词 however。

5. 选 O) 他必须适应管理严密的大学系统, 而这一点是与他国内的管理大不相同的。that 是指代严密的管理。

6. 选 K) 所有外来教授和他的学生都缺乏共同的文化共同性。

7. 选 G) 外来教授需要接受那些已在美国学生头脑里已存在的概念。

8. 选 J) 做些调整用动词 make。大学必须做出适当的调整。

9. 选 E) offer 意思是"提供, 供应"。

10. 选 A) field 意思是"领域"。这是一个有待进一步研究的领域。

第五节　篇章阅读理解模拟训练——应试难度

特训一及答案

▶Passage one

Nearly two thousand years have passed since a census decreed by Caesar Augustus become part of the greatest story ever told. Many things have changed in the intervening years. The hotel industry worries more about overbuilding than overcrowding, and if they had to meet an unexpected influx, few inns would have a manager to accommodate the weary guests.

Now it is the census taker that does the traveling in the fond hope that a highly mobile population will stay long enough to get a good sampling. Methods of gathering, recording, and evaluating information have presumably been improved a great deal. And where then it was the modest purpose of Rome to obtain a simple head count as an adequate basis for levying taxes, now batteries of complicated statistical series furnished by governmental agencies and private organizations are eagerly scanned and interpreted by sages and seers to get a clue to future events. The Bible does not tell us how the Roman census takers made out, and as regards our more immediate concern, the reliability of present day economic forecasting, there are considerable differences of opinion. They were aired at the celebration of the 125th anniversary of the American Statistical Association. There was the thought that business forecasting might well be on its way from an art to a science, and some speakers talked about newfangled computers and high-falutin mathematical system in terms of excitement and endearment which we, at least in our younger years when these things mattered, would have associated more readily with the description of a fair maiden. But others pointed to the deplorable record of highly esteemed forecasts and forecasters with a batting average below that of the Mets, and the President-elect of the Association cautioned that "high powered statistical methods are usually in order where the facts are crude and inadequate, the exact contrary of what crude and inadequate statisticians assume."

We left his birthday party somewhere between hope and despair and with the conviction, not really newly acquired, that proper statistical methods applied to ascertainable facts have their merits in economic forecasting as long as neither forecaster nor public is deluded into mistaking the delineation of probabilities and trends for a prediction of certainties of mathematical exactitude.

1. Taxation in Roman days apparently was based on _____.

   A) wealth　B) mobility　C) population　D) census takers

2. The American Statistical Association _____.

   A) is converting statistical study from an art to a science

   B) has an excellent record in business forecasting

   C) is neither hopeful nor pessimistic

   D) speaks with mathematical exactitude

3. The message the author wishes the reader to get is _____.

   A) statisticians have not advanced since the days of the Roman

   B) statistics is not as yet a science

   C) statisticians love their machine

   D) computer is hopeful

4. The "greatest story ever told" referred to in the passage is the story of _____.

   A) Christmas　　　　　　B) The Mets

   C) Moses　　　　　　　　D) Roman Census Takers

▶**Passage two**

Moreover, insofar as any interpretation of its author can be made from the five or six plays attributed to him, the Wakefield Master is uniformly considered to be a man of sharp contemporary observation. He was, formally, perhaps clerically educated, as his Latin and music, his Biblical and patristic lore indicate. He is, still, celebrated mainly for his quick sympathy for the oppressed and forgotten man, his sharp eye for character, a ready ear for colloquial vernacular turns of speech and a humor alternately rude and boisterous, coarse and happy. Hence despite his conscious artistry as manifest in his feeling for intricate metrical and stanza forms, he is looked upon as a kind of medieval Steinbeck, indignantly angry at, uncompromisingly and even brutally realistic in presenting the plight of the agricultural poor.

Thus taking the play and the author together, it is now fairly conventional to regard the former as a kind of ultimate point in the secularization of the medieval drama. Hence much emphasis on it as depicting realistically humble manners and pastoral life in the bleak hills of the West Riding of Yorkshire on a typically cold night of December 24th. After what are often regarded as almost "documentaries" given in the three successive monologues of the three shepherds, critics go on to affirm that the realism is then intensified into a burlesque mock-treatment of the Nativity. Finally as a sort of epilogue or after-thought in deference to the Biblical origins of the materials, the play slides back into an atavistic mood of early innocent reverence. Actually, as we shall see, the final scene is not only the culminating scene but perhaps the raison d'etre of introductory "realism".

There is much on the surface of the present play to support the conventional view of its mood of secular realism. All the same, the "realism" of the Wakefield Master is of a paradoxical turn. His wide knowledge of people, as well as books indicates no cloistered contemplative but one in close relation to his times. Still, that life was after all a predominantly religious one, a time which never neglected the belief that man was a rebellious and sinful creature in need of redemption, So deeply (one can hardly say "naively" of so sophisticated a writer) and implicitly religious is the Master that he is less able（or less willing）to present actual history realistically than is the author of the Brome "Abraham and Isaac". His historical sense is even less realistic than that of Chaucer who just a few years before had done for his own time costume romances, such as The Knight's Tale, Troilus and Cressida, etc. Moreover Chaucer had the excuse of highly romantic materials for taking liberties with history.

1. Which of the following statements about the Wakefield Master is NOT True?

 A）He was Chaucer's contemporary.

 B）He is remembered as the author of five or six realistic plays.

 C）He write like John Steinbeck.

 D）HE was an accomplished artist.

2. By "patristic", the author means _____.

 A）realistic

 B）patriotic

 C）superstitious

 D）pertaining to the Christian Fathers

3. The statement about the "secularization of the medieval drama" refers to the _____.

 A）introduction of mundane matters in religious plays

 B）presentation of erudite material

 C）use of contemporary introduction of religious themes in the early days

 D）The historical sese on some fomous people

4. In subsequent paragraphs, we may expect the writer of this passage to _____.

 A）justify his comparison with Steinbeck

 B）present a point of view which attack the thought of the second paragraph

C）point out the anachronisms in the play

D）discuss the works of Chaucer

答案

▶**Passage one**

解析：

1. 选 C）。人口。答案在第六句，"那时罗马计算人头作为征税的适当基础，目的很简单。"

   A）财富；B）流动性；C）人口调查员。

2. 选 A）。正把统计研究从文科转变成理科。这是从第六句开始讲的一种观点。"现在，政府机构和私人组织的一系列复杂的统计数字，由智者和先知人物殷切地浏览和解释以取得预知未来事件的线索。圣经并没有告诉我们罗马的人口调查员是怎么调查统计的。至于我们当前更加关心的问题：目前经济预测的可靠性，意见分歧很大。美国统计协会 125 周年庆祝活动上，人们在大肆宣扬这些不同观点。有一种说法是经济预测可能正从文科转向科学（理科）发展。有些人兴高采烈大谈新型计算机和高级数学系统。"作者虽然没有明说，明眼人一看便知，艺术向科学转变正是美国统计协会在把统计学从文科转向理科。所以 A）对。

   B）在商业预测方面具有杰出的记录，不对，实际上"平均成功率还低于 the Mets"；C）既没有希望也不乐观，文内没有提及，只提作者他们半喜半忧离开协会；D）以数学的精确性来说话。见下道题解释。协会部分人却有此看法"数学精确性。"

3. 选 B）。统计学（到现在为止）还不是一门科学（理科）。文章的倒数第二段的最后也表明："连统计协会的主席也告诫说高能统计法在实际材料原始和不允许的地方一般发挥正常。而文章的最后也交待了一些关于对统计，统计员之间的期望。"

   A）统计员从罗马时代起就没向前进步过；C）统计员爱计算机，这两项文内没有提到；D）计算机前程远大。文内只讲了有些人怀着兴高采烈的心情大讲新型计算机和高级数学"系统"，暗示了计算机大有希望。但不是所有人都这样认为的。最重要的是计算机的应用并不能改变这个事实：统计学不是理科，而是文科。所以 B) 对。

4. 选 A)。基督，圣诞节，指基督的诞生。圣经中的一个故事。

B) the Mets. 圣经中率领希伯莱人出埃及的领袖，也作放债的犹太人讲；C) 摩西；D) 罗马人口调查员。

▶**Passage two**

解析：

1. 选 C)。他像斯坦贝克一样写作。第一段作者说他是一位公认的对当代具有敏锐洞察力的作家。现在仍然享有盛名。主要体现在第一段中间的部分：He is, still, celebrated … the plight of the agricultural poor，整段话说明，文内两位作家之共同点是在内容观点上。而不是指一样的艺术形式上。韦克菲尔写的是诗歌形式——韵文，而斯坦贝克是小说和散文剧。所以说他像斯坦贝克那样写作就错了。故选 C)。

A) 他是乔叟同时代的人，见最后一句"他对历史观点的现实主义稍逊于乔叟。乔叟在几年前就为其时代写了一本传奇。"；B) 他是作为五或六本现实剧本的作者而为人纪念。本文第一句话"只能从他写的五个或六个剧本来说明这位作者。"；D) 他是一位有成就的艺术家。

2. 选 D)。Patristic 意为关于早期基督教领袖的。第一段中 his Biblical and Patristic lore indicate 的意思是"他那有关圣经和早期基督教领袖们的歌谣。"

A) 现实主义的；B) 爱国的；C) 迷信的。

3. 选 A)。在宗教剧中介绍世俗之事。见第二段中的 secularization 意为："世俗化、脱离教会"。这一整段都讲了韦剧中对世俗之事的描述："拿剧本和作者两者一起讲的话，现在习惯于把他的剧本看作中世纪戏剧世俗化的一个顶点。因此，对他世俗化强调常以一个例子来说明，即他现实主义的描述 12 月 24 日一个寒冷的夜晚，在约克郡西区荒凉的山里的那种粗陋的习俗和乡村的生活；在常被人认为几乎是'记录文献'的三个牧人三段连续的独白之后，批评家们继续认为他的现实主义在此时被强化到以讽刺嘲弄的口吻处理了基督的诞生。最后，作者收场白或事后的补充，对材料的来源圣经表示敬意。剧本又滑回到早期纯洁无邪（天真）的崇敬，一种返祖基调中去。事实上最后一幕不仅是全剧的高潮，也许还是'现实主义'引言存在的理由。"这一段清楚表明。批评者认为宗教只是作者的收场白，计划外的添加剂而已。

B）表现渊博知识材料；C）应用当代材料，太笼统，当代也有宗教之事；D）介绍早期宗教题材。

4. 选 B）。表达抨击第二段思想的观点。这个问题最难回答，其所以选择 B）是因为本人作者并不同意流行的观点。他在讲完"常规看法"后，用引导来谈"纪实文献"和"现实主义"。这说明作者的含义并不是这两个词的本义。这段最后一句话"事实上，最后一幕……"表明最后一幕有宗教内容，而"现实主义"不过处于 introductory 阶段。第三段点明作者的观点"现在的戏剧表面上有许多支持世俗现实主义模式的观点"。韦之"现实主义"有一个自相矛盾的特点。他对人和书本广泛的了解表明"他不是与世隔绝，而是和时代紧密相连的。再说，那时的生活毕竟是全方位的宗教。那时代绝不会忽视这种信仰——人是叛逆和有罪的生灵，需要赎罪。大师是那么深沉含蓄的信奉宗教，因而他比布罗姆作者更不可能（更不愿）现实主义地表现真正的历史。他的历史感现实性甚至比乔叟更不现实主义。乔叟早在前几年为他的时代写了'类似'骑士的故事、特罗依拉斯和克莱西德等传奇。再说，乔叟以高度浪漫的材料为借口对历史事实任意处理。"所以说，我们可以期望作者在下面一步发挥自己的观点，抨击第二段的看法。

A）他和斯坦贝克的比较是公平的；C）指出剧中时代错误；D）讨论乔叟作品。

特训二及答案

▶**Passage one**

In a family where the roles of men and women are not sharply separated and where many household tasks are shared to a greater or lesser extent, notions of male superiority are hard to maintain. The pattern of sharing in tasks and indecision makes for equality and this in turn leads to further sharing. In such a home, the growing boy and girl learn to accept equality more easily than did their parents and to prepare more fully for participation in a world characterized by cooperation rather than by the "battle of the sexes"。

If the process goes too far and man's role is regarded as less important — and that has happened in some cases — we are as badly off as before, only in reverse.

It is time to reassess the role of the man in the American family. We are getting a little tired of "Momism" — but we don't want to exchange it for a "neo-Popism"。What we need, rather, is the recognition that bringing up children involves a partnership of equals. There are signs that psychiatrists, psychologists, social workers, and specialists on the family are becoming more aware of the part men play and that they have decided that women should not receive all the credit — nor the blame. We have almost given up saying that a woman's place is in the home. We are beginning, however, to analyze man's place in the home and to insist that he does have a place in it. Nor is that place irrelevant to the healthy development of the child.

The family is a co-operative enterprise for which it is difficult to lay down rules, because each family needs to work out its own ways for solving its own problems.

Excessive authoritarianism （命令主义） has unhappy consequences, whether it wears skirts or trousers, and the ideal of equal rights and equal responsibilities is pertinent （相关的，切题的） not only to a healthy democracy, but also to a healthy family.

1. The ideal of equal rights and equal responsibilities is _____.

　　A）fundamental to a sound democracy

　　B）not pertinent to healthy family life

C) responsible for Momism

D) what we have almost given up

2. The danger in the sharing of household tasks by the mother and the father is that _____.

A) the role of the father may become an inferior one

B) the role of the mother may become an inferior one

C) the children will grow up believing that life is a battle of sexes

D) sharing leads to constant arguing

3. The author states that bringing up children _____.

A) is mainly the mother's job

B) belongs among the duties of the father

C) is the job of schools and churches

D) involves a partnership of equals

4. According to the author, the father's role in the home is _____.

A) minor because he is an ineffectual parent

B) irrelevant to the healthy development of the child

C) pertinent to the healthy development of the child

D) identical to the role of the child's mother

5. With which of the following statements would the author be most likely to agree?

A) A healthy, co-operative family is a basic ingredient of a healthy society.

B) Men are basically opposed to sharing household chores.

C) Division of household responsibilities is workable only in theory.

D) A woman's place in the home — now as always.

答案

解析:

1. 选 A) 对一个健全的民主很重要。文章的最后一段的后半句是本文的主题句，它明确说 the ideal of equal rights and equal responsibilities is pertinent (相关的，切题的) not only to a healthy

democracy, but also to a healthy family, 此处的 pertinent 与题干中的 fundamental 在此处的意思是一样的。

2. 选 A）父亲的角色很可能变的不那么重要了。本题较难，表面是个细节题，但实际是推断题。有两处线索：第一处是第二段的第一句话，该句承接第一段中谈论的 sharing household，指出如果过分了的话，就会导致男人被认为较不重要，即是选项 A）的意思。第二处线索是第三段的倒数第二句话中 "… that he does have a place in it"。

3. 选 D）涉及到平等的合作关系。线索见第三段的第二句话 What we need, rather, is the recognition that bringing up children involves a partnership of equals.

4. 选 C）与孩子健康的成长有关系。本题的线索与第 1 题是一样的。

5. 选 A）一个健康的，互相合作的家庭是健康的社会里是很重要的成分。本题除了用排除法做以外，仍然考的是主题句。最后一句中的 a healthy democracy 是从社会的角度来讲的。

▶Passage two

Teaching children to read well from the start is the most important task of elementary schools. But relying on educators to approach this task correctly can be a great mistake. Many schools continue to employ instructional methods that have been proven ineffective. The staying power of the "look-say" or "whole-word" method of teaching beginning reading is perhaps the most flagrant example of this failure to instruct effectively.

The whole-word approach to reading stresses the meaning of words over the meaning of letters, thinking over decoding, developing a sight vocabulary of familiar words over developing the ability to unlock the pronunciation of unfamiliar words. It fits in with the self-directed, "learning how to learn" activities recommended by advocates（倡导者）of "open" classrooms and with the concept that children have to be developmentally ready to begin reading. Before 1963, no major publisher put out anything but these "Run-Spot-Run" readers.

However, in 1955, Rudolf Flesch touched off what has been called "the great debate" in beginning reading. In his best-seller Why Johnny Can't Read, Flesch indicted（控诉）the nation's public schools for mis-educating students by using the look-say method. He said — and more scholarly studies by Jeane Chall and Rovert Dykstra later confirmed — that another approach to beginning reading, founded on phonics（语音学）, is far superior.

Systematic phonics first teachers children to associate letters and letter combinations with sounds; it then teaches them how to blend these sounds together to make words. Rather than building up a relatively limited vocabulary of memorized words, it imparts a code by which the pronunciations of the vast majority of the most common words in the English language can be learned. Phonics does not devalue the importance of thinking about the meaning of words and sentences; it simply recognizes that decoding is the logical and necessary first step.

1. The author feels that counting on educators to teach reading correctly is _____.

    A) only logical and natural

    B) the expected position

    C) probably a mistake

    D) merely effective instruction

2. The author indicts the look-say reading approach because _____.

    A) it overlooks decoding

    B) Rudolf Flesch agrees with him

    C) he says it is boring

    D) many schools continue to use this method

3. One major difference between the look-say method of learning reading and the phonics method is _____.

    A) look-say is simpler

B）Phonics takes longer to learn

C）look-say is easier to teach

D）phonics gives readers access to far more words

4. The phrase "touch-off"（Para 3, Line 1）most probably means _____.

A）talk about shortly

B）start or cause

C）compare with

D）oppose

5. According to the author, which of the following statements is true?

A）Phonics approach regards whole-word method as unimportant.

B）The whole-word approach emphasizes decoding.

C）In phonics approach, it is necessary and logical to employ decoding.

D）Phonics is superior because it stresses the meaning of words thus the vast majority of most common words can be learned.

答案

解析：

1. 选 C）可能是个错误。本题的线索是第一段的第二句话，其中的 relying on educators 与题干中的 counting on educators 完全是同样的意思。

2. 选 A）忽略了解码。作者先在第一段的最后一句说"look-say"或"whole-word"的阅读教学方法是失败的，第二段分析了这种方法失败的原因，是因为它"stresses the meaning of words over the meaning of letters, thinking over decoding…"

3. 选 D）声学让读者可以学习更多的单词。文章在最后一段谈到了 phonics method 的特点和好处，本题线索见该段的第二句话"Rather than building up a relatively limited vocabulary of memorized words, it imparts a code by which the pronunciations of the vast majority of the most common words in the English language can be learned"，可见这种方法能使学习者获得更大的词汇量。

4. 选 B）开始或引起。本题要求利用上下文猜测单词的意思。根据第二段的最后一句，在 1963 年以前，出版的东西都是教授使用 whole-word 的方法的，紧接着用了转折词 however，说在 1955 年，Rudolf Flesch "touched off" 一场争论，因此此处的 touch off 必然是"引起"的意思。

5. 选 C）在声学的学习上，采用解码是很必要和有逻辑性的。本题要求有较好的综合能力才能做得既快又准。从第二段中综合出 whole-word 阅读方法的特点：强调单词的意思、没有 decoding；由此即可知 B）、D）是错的；在文章的最后一句话，作者指出 Phonics does not devalue the importance of thinking about the meaning of words and sentences，所以 A）也是不对的。

特训三及答案

▶Passage one

Shams and delusions are esteemed for soundest truths, while reality is fabulous. If men would steadily observe realities only, and not allow themselves to be deluded, life, to compare it with such things as we know, would be like a fairy tale and the Arabian Nights' Entertainments. If we respected only what is inevitable and has a right to be, music and poetry would resound along the streets. When we are unhurried and wise, we perceive that only great and worthy things have any permanent and absolute existence, — that petty fears and petty pleasure are but the shadow of reality. This is always exhilarating and sublime. By closing the eyes and slumbering, by consenting to be deceived by shows, men establish and confirm their daily life of routine and habit everywhere, which still is built on purely illusory foundation. Children, who play life, discern its true law and relations more clearly than men, who fail to live worthily, but who think that they are wiser by experience, that is, by failure. I have read in a Hindoo book, that "there was a king's son, who, being expelled in infancy from his native city, was brought up by a forester, and, growing up to maturity in that state, imagined himself to belong to the barbarous race with which be lived. One of his father's ministers having discovered him, revealed to him what he was, and the misconception of his character was removed, and he knew himself to be a prince. So soul, from the circumstances in which it is placed, mistakes its own character, until the truth is revealed to it by some holy teacher, and then it knows itself to be Brahme." We think that that is which appears to be. If a man should give us an account of the realities he beheld, we should not recognize the place in his description. Look at a meeting-house, or a court-house, or a jail, or a shop. Or a dwelling-house, and say what that thing really is before a true gaze, and they would all go to pieces in your account of them. Men esteem truth remote, in the outskirts of the system, behind the farthest star, before Adam and after the last man. In eternity there is indeed something true and sublime. But all these times and places and occasions are now and here. God himself culminates in the present moment, and will never be more divine in the lapse of all ages. And we are enabled to apprehend at all what is sublime and noble only by the perpetual instilling and drenching of the reality that surrounds us. The universe constantly and obediently answers to our conceptions; whether we travel fast or slow, the track is laid for us. Let us spend our lives in conceiving then. The poet or the artist never yet had as fair and noble a design but some of his posterity at least could accomplish it.

1. The writer's attitude toward the arts is one of _____.

    A) admiration B) indifference C) suspicion D) repulsion

2. The author believes that a child _____.

    A) should practice what the Hindoos preach

    B) frequently faces vital problems better than grownups do

    C) hardly ever knows his true origin

    D) is incapable of appreciating the arts

3. The author is primarily concerned with urging the reader to _____.

A) look to the future for enlightenment

B) appraise the present for its true value

C) honor the wisdom of the past ages

D) spend more time in leisure activities

4. The passage is primarily concerned with problem of _____.

A) history and economics   B) society and population

C) biology and physics   D) theology and philosophy

▶**Passage two**

The origin of continental nuclei has long been a puzzle. Theories advanced so far have generally failed to explain the first step in continent growth, or have been subject to serious objections. It is the purpose of this article to examine the possible role of the impact of large meteorites or asteroids in the production of continental nuclei. Unfortunately, the geological evolution of the Earth's surface has had an obliterating effect on the original composition and structure of the continents to such an extent that further terrestrial investigations have small chance of arriving at an unambiguous answer to the question of continental origin. Paradoxically, clues to the origin and early history of the surface features of the Earth may be found on the Moon and planets, rather than on the Earth, because some of these bodies appear to have had a much less active geological history. As a result, relatively primitive surface features are preserved for study and analysis. In the case of both the Moon and Mars, it is generally concluded from the appearance of their heavily cratered surfaces that they have been subjected to bombardment by large meteoroids during their geological history. Likewise, it would appear a reasonable hypothesis that the Earth has also been subjected to meteoroid bombardment in the past, and that very large bodies struck the Earth early in its geological history.

The large crater on the Moon listed by Baldwin has a diameter of 285 km. However, if we accept the hypotheses of formation of some of the mare basins by impact, the maximum lunar impact crater diameter is probably as large as 650km. Based on a lunar analogy, one might expect several impact craters of at least 500km diameter to have been formed on Earth. By applying Baldwin's equation, the depth of such a crater should be about 20km. Baldwin admits that his equation gives excessive depths for large craters so that the actual depth should be somewhat smaller. Based on the measured depth of smaller lunar crater. Baldwin's equation gives the depth of the zone of brecciation for such a crater as about 75km. The plasticity of the Earth's mantle at the depth makes it impossible to speak of "bracciation" in the usual sense. However, local stresses may be temporarily sustained at that depth, as shown by the existence of deep-focus earthquakes. Thus, short-term effects might be expected to a depth of more than 50km in the mantle.

Even without knowing the precise effects, there is little doubt that the formation of a 500 km crater would be a major geological event. Numerous authors have considered the geological implications of such an event. Donn et al. have, for example, called on the impact of continent-size bodies of sialic composition to from the original continents. Two major difficulties inherent in this concept are the lack of any known sialic meteorites, and the high probability that the energy of impact would result in a wide dissemination of sialic material, rather than its concentration at the point of impact.

Gilvarry, on the other hand, called on meteoroid impact to explain the production of ocean basins. The major difficulties with this model are that the morphology of most of the ocean basins is not consistent with impact, and that the origin and growth of continents is not adequately explained.

We agree with Donn at al. that the impact of large meteorites or asteroids may have caused continent formation, but would rather think in terms of the localized addition of energy to the system, rather than in terms of the addition of actual sialic material.

1. A mare basin is _____.

   A) a formula for determining the relationship between the depth and width of craters

   B) a valley that is filled in when a spatial body has impact with the moon or the earth

   C) a planetoid (small planet) created when a meteorite, upon striking the moon, breaks off a part of the moon

   D) a dark spot on the moon, once supposed to be a sea, now a plain

2. The writer does not believe that _____.

   A) an asteroid is larger than a meteorite

   B) material from space, upon hitting the earth, was eventually distributed

   C) the earth, at one time, had craters

   D) ocean were formerly craters

3. The article is primarily concerned with _____.

   A) the origin of continents

   B) the relationship between astral phenomena and the moon

   C) differences of opinion among authoritative geologists

   D) the relationship between asteroids and meteorites

4. Sialic material refers to _____.

   A) the broken rock resulting from the impact of a meteorite against the earth

   B) material that exists on planets other than the earth

   C) a composite of rock typical of continental areas of the earth

   D) material that is man-made to simulate materials that existed far back in geological history

答案

▶**Passage one**

解析：

1. 选 A）。钦佩。本文第三句"如果我们只尊重必然的东西，尊重有权威为必然的东西，那么音乐和诗歌会重新在街上唱诵。"本文最后一句"虽然诗人或艺术从来没有如此美好和崇高的设想，但他们有些后代至少会达到这一步的。"这些都说明作者对艺术视为崇高和美好，不是被蒙蔽的东西。

B）漠不关心；C）怀疑的；D）排斥。都不对。

2. 选 B）。孩子们常常比成人更好地面对各种问题。本文第七句"孩子们游戏生活（整天只知道玩儿），却比难以很好生活的成人们更清楚的分辨出显示生活的真正规律和种种关系。"

A）孩子应当实践印度教宣传的东西；C）几乎对其真实出身一无所知，这是讲王子的事情，不是一般孩子；D）难以欣赏艺术。并未提及。

3. 选 B）。珍视目前的真正价值。这在文章倒数第五句作者主要是为了强调现实才是人们应该抓住的。

A）指望未来给予启迪；C）尊重过去的智慧；D）在悠闲的活动中花更多的时间。

4. 选 D）。神学和哲学。整篇文章都传递了这两个内容，特别是哲学推理说。

A）历史和经济学；B）社会和人口；C）生物和物理。

▶Passage two

解析：

1. 选 D）。是月球上的一个黑点，一度认识是海，现在知道是平原。mare basin"海盆地"。词意本身说明 D）项对。另一方面，第二段开始提及"鲍德温所列出的月球上最大的陨石坑直径为 285 公里。可是，如果我们接受了某些由于撞击而形成海盆地的结构假设，那么月球上最大陨石坑的直径可能有 650 公里。"这里都说mare basin 指的是月球上陨石坑。这就排除了 A）、B）、C）三个选项。

A）是测定陨石坑深度和宽度的公式；B）当某一天体或地球撞击时填入的深谷；C）当陨星撞击月亮时，撞掉的部分月亮而形成小星体。

2. 选 D）。海洋是原来的陨石坑。倒数第二段"另一方面，Gilvarry 用陨星撞击来解释海洋盆地的形成。这一模式的最大困难在于大多数海洋盆地结构和撞击情况不符。"

A）小行星大于陨星；B）来自太空的材料，在撞击地球时，均匀分布；C）地球一度有过陨石坑。这三项明显不对，谈不上相信不相信。

3. 选 A）。大陆起源。这在文章一开始就点明"大陆核起源长期以来一直是个谜。进展到现在的理论一般都不能说明大陆生长的第一步情况，或者遭到严厉的反对。这篇文章的目的就是要研究大陨星或小行星的撞击在地球核生成中可能起的作用。"

B）星际现象和月球的关系；C）权威地质学家意见分歧；D）小行星和陨星之间的关系。

4. 选 C）。地球大陆地区特有的岩石构成。第三段第三句："举例说，Donn et al. 提出大陆区域大小的，硅铝结构的天体撞击形成最初的大陆块的设想。"

A）由于陨星撞击地球形成破碎的岩石；B）存在于地球之外其他星球的材料；C）人造材料模拟存在于遥远地质史上的材料。三项文内都没有提到。

特训四及答案

▶Passage one

In cities with rent control, the city government sets the maximum rent that a landlord can charge for an apartment. Supporters of rent control argue that it protects people who are living in apartments. Their rent cannot increase; therefore, they are not in danger of losing their homes. However, the critics say that after a long time, rent control may have negative effects. Landlords know that they cannot increase their profits. Therefore, they invest in other businesses where they can increase their profits. They do not invest in new buildings which would also be rent-controlled. As a result, new apartments are not built. Many people who need apartments cannot find any. According to the critics, the end result of rent control is a shortage of apartments in the city.

Some theorists argue that the minimum wage law can cause problems in the same way. The federal government sets the minimum that an employer must pay workers. The minimum helps people who generally look for unskilled, low-paying jobs. However, if the minimum is high, employers may hire fewer workers. They will replace workers with machinery. The price, which is the wage that employers must pay, increases. Therefore, other things being equal, the number of workers that employers want decreases. Thus, critics claim, an increase in the minimum wage may cause unemployment. Some poor people may find themselves without jobs instead of with jobs at the minimum wage.

Supporters of the minimum wage say that it helps people keep their dignity. Because of the law, workers cannot sell their services for less than the minimum. Furthermore, employers cannot force workers to accept jobs at unfair wages.

Economic theory predicts the results of economic decisions such as decisions about farm production, rent control, and the minimum wage. The predictions may be correct only if " other things are equal ". Economists do not agree on some of the predictions. They also do not agree on the value of different decisions. Some economists support a particular decision while others criticize it. Economists do agree, however, that there are no simple answers to economic questions.

1. There is the possibility that setting maximum rent may _____.

   A) cause a shortage of apartments

   B) worry those who rent apartments as homes

   C) increase the profits of landlords

   D) encourage landlords to invest in building apartment

2. According to the critics, rent control _____.

   A) will always benefit those who rent apartments

   B) is unnecessary

C) will bring negative effects in the long run

D) is necessary under all circumstances

3. The problem of unemployment will arise _____.

A) if the minimum wage is set too high

B) if the minimum wage is set too low

C) if the workers are unskilled

D) if the maximum wage is set

4. The passage tells us _____.

A) the relationship between supply and demand

B) the possible results of government controls

C) the necessity of government control

D) the urgency of getting rid of government controls

5. Which of the following statements is NOT true?

A) The results of economic decisions can not always be predicted.

B) Minimum wage can not always protect employees.

C) Economic theory can predict the results of economic decisions if other factors are not changing.

D) Economic decisions should not be based on economic theory.

▶**Passage two**

For a thousand years and more, the people of Europe had fought about many things, but they had been united in believing one thing: that there existed a single "Holy, Catholic and Apostolic Church" of which the Bishop of Rome, under the title of the Pope, was the visible and recognizable head in succession to St. Peter. But in 1517 a German monk, Martin Luther, challenged certain Catholic teachings and renounced his obedience to the papacy. Others had followed him, including Henry VIII.

Thus Europe was divided in every which way, the southern and eastern two-thirds still Catholic, the northern and western one-third what was coming to be called Protestant, though English-ruled Ireland solidly Catholic and the Spanish-ruled Netherlands, particularly the northern part approximating to modern Holland, grew increasingly Protestant; while in virtually every country, whether officially Catholic or Protestant, those of the contrary faith fiercely attempted to convert their neighbors and equally fiercely resisted their neighbor's attempts to convert them. For this there was no simple, friendly solution to be reached on the principle of live-and-let-live. Each party believed that it had hold of the truth, the only truth that mattered, the one that led to eternal salvation, and its adversaries clung to falsehood which must necessarily head to eternal damnation: not only for themselves but for all who should permit them to survive and infect others with their errors. Toleration, even reasonable discussion, was impossible. God and the devil could not mix. Just as Elizabeth was to ardent Catholics that Jezebel, so to earnest Protestants the Pope was "that wolfish bloodsucker," and their Catholic fellow-creatures mad dogs, toads and other such vermin to be cleansed off the face of the earth.

These feelings, dangerous enough in themselves, were made more so by questions of geography and money. The Catholic countries bordering on the Mediterranean were by far the richest. From the beginning of the Middle Ages the Republic of Venice had controlled the trade routes to the East, bringing the wares carried out of Persia, China and the Indies by camel to her depots in Syria and reloading them in her high, gorgeously painted vessels for transshipment to Italy and beyond. Since the end of the fifteen century, first Portugal by sailing round Africa to India, then Spain by the discovery of America, had likewise been in a position to bring for sale to Europe all the rare and wonderful things for which Europe longed — silks and precious woods, sugar and spices, gold and silver, works of exquisite art and strange animals from peacock to tigers. In 1494, two years after Columbus's first voyage to America, Pope Alexander VI had divided the unexplored world beyond the seas between Spain and Portugal as reward for their enterprise and to keep them from fighting. The other countries had respected this division so long as they remained

Catholic.

1. The best title for this passage is _____.

   A) The History of Europe in 16th Century

   B) The Religious History of Europe in 16th Century

   C) The Causes of European Separation in 16th Century

   D) The Factors of European Separation in the 16th century

2. What does we learn from the passage?

   A) The Pope had the supreme power in religion before reform.

   B) The Pope had the greatest power in every thing outside religion.

   C) The Pope was the real king in Europe then.

   D) The Pope was the real ruler in Europe then.

3. What did the sentence "The other countries had respected this division so long as they remained Catholic" imply?

   A) It implied this division could not be respected long.

   B) It implied this division would not face a challenge.

   C) It implied this division would be respected forever.

   D) It implied the power of the Pope would never decline.

4. Which of the following is not mentioned as a cause to deepen the dangerous feelings?

   A) Money.　　B) Geology.　　C) Religion.　　D) Geography.

▶**Passage one**

解析：

1. 选 A）。引起公寓的短缺。本文章第一段明确指出，landlords（房东）收取租户的租金有了最高限额，他们的利润会受到影响，也可能导致他们投资其他行业，鉴于此，C）、D）两项都是错误的。B）项"使租房为家的人担忧"文中没有涉及，也不对。依据第一段最后一句话"…, the end result of rent control is a shortage of apartments in the city."可知 A 项为惟一选项。

2. 选 C）。从长远看会带来一些负面影响。依据第一段第四句"However, the critics say that after a long time, rent control may have

negative effects. "可断定 C) 项正确。A)、B)、D) 诸项都含绝对意味，都不符合文中意思。

3. 选 A)。如果最低工资设置的太高。解答该题只要准确理解第二段的含义，尤其从第三行开始 "However, if the minimum is high，… Thus，critics claim，an increase in the minimum wage may cause unemployment. "此题较简单。

4. 选 B)。政府控制造成的可能后果。本文从 rent control 和最低工资控制两方面讨论了政府控制可能造成的后果。进一步说，许多政府行为可能保护某些利益，但从长远看，也会带来许多问题。B) 项正确。A) 项说（文章叙述了）供需关系；C) 项说（文章叙述了）政府控制的必要性；D) 项说（文章叙述了）摆脱政府控制的紧迫性。文章并没有深入谈及这三项内容，显然不能成为文章主旨。

5. 选 D)。经济性决策不能以经济性理论为基础。依据第四段第二行 "The predictions may be correct only if 'other things are equal'. "可得知 A) 项是对的。从第二段可得知规定最低工资会使得雇主雇用更少的工人，会考虑用机器替代工人，也就会导致更多的人失业，所以 B) 项应该是可以成立的说法。C) 项的内容实际上就是 A) 项的另一种说法，也可成立。依据第四段内容，可得知 D) 项不正确。经济理论应该有相当的参考价值，只是还需考虑方方面面的因素。

▶Passage two

解析：

1. 选 D)。16 世纪欧洲分裂的因素。上面文章大意中作者是从三方面论及其分裂。第三段第一句："这些情感，本身就危险，再加上地理和金钱两个问题，情况就更加不妙了。"

A) 欧洲史；B) 欧洲宗教史，这两项涉及面更广；C) 宗教改革对 16 世纪欧洲的影响。和标题有些接近。但第三段却是和宗教无关的两个因素。

2. 选 C)。在改革前，罗马教皇是欧洲真正的帝王。这在第一段中有明确的叙述"一千多年来,欧洲的人们虽然在许多事情彼此斗争过,可是在信仰上团结一致,都信只有一个神圣的天主教和罗马教皇的教会。那里的罗马大主教,称为教皇,是继承圣·彼德之后有形的公认领袖。可是,1517年德国僧侣,马丁·路德向某些天主教教义提出挑衅,拒绝服从罗马教皇,以及追随他,其中包括亨利八世(英王)"。

A)在改革前,罗马教皇在宗教上具有至高无上的权利。似乎很有道理,实际上,教皇虽是宗教领袖,管的事情远远超出宗教范畴。这在最后一段倒数第二句话可见一般,结合第三题谈;B)教皇在宗教之外的许多事情有着最高的权利,是明显不对的;D)教皇是那时欧洲的真正统治者。Then 一词可以指改革前后。

3. 选 A)。这种分割不可能长期得到尊重。最后一段的最后两句话 "1494年,哥伦布首次远航美洲后的两年,教皇亚历山大六世就把这块大洋彼岸未曾勘探的世界分给西班牙和葡萄牙作为对他们业绩的褒奖(赏赐)和制止他们彼此开仗。其他国家只要他们依然信仰天主教,他们就会尊重这个瓜分。"as long as 是一个条件。一旦这个条件不存在,那就不会再尊重。另一方面也说明教皇不仅管宗教,见第2题 A 注释,因此并不正确。

B. 不会面临挑战。C. 永远得到尊重。D. 教皇权力永不衰退。

4. 选 B)。地质学。A)钱;C)宗教;D)地理位置。都提到过。

第六节　篇章阅读理解模拟训练——拔高难度

特训一及答案

▶Passage one

Old people are always saying that the young are not what they were. The same comment is made from generation to generation and it is always true. It has never been truer than it is today. The young are better educated. They have a lot more money to spend and enjoy more freedom.

They grow up more quickly and are not so dependent on their parents. They think more for themselves and do not blindly accept the ideals of their elders. Events which the older generation remembers vividly are nothing more than past history. This is as it should be. Every new generation is different from the one that preceded it. Today the difference is very marked indeed.

The old always assume that they know best for the simple reason that they have been around a bit longer. They don't like to feel that their values are being questioned or threatened. And this is precisely what the young are doing. They are question the assumptions of their elders and disturbing their complacency. Office hours, for instance, are nothing more than enforced slavery. Wouldn't people work best if they were given complete freedom and responsibility? And what about clothing? Who said that all the men in the world should wear drab grey suits and convict haircuts? If we ruin our minds to more serious matters, who said that human differences can best be solved through conventional politics or by violent means, who said that human difference can best be solved through conventional politics or by violent means? Why have the older generation so often used violence to solve their problems? Why are they so unhappy and guilt-ridden in their personal lives, so obsessed with mean ambitions and the desire to amass more and more material possessions? Can anything be right with the rat-race? Haven't the old lost touch with all that is important in life?

These are not questions the older generation can shrug off lightly. Their record over the past forty years or so hasn't been exactly spotless. Traditionally, the young have turned to their elders for guidance. Today, the situation might be reversed. The old — if they are prepared to admit it — could learn a thing or two from their children. One of the biggest lessons they could learn is that enjoyment is not 'sinful'. Enjoyment is a principle one could apply to all aspects of life. It is surely not wrong to enjoy your work and enjoy your leisure; to shed restricting inhibitions. It is surely not wrong to live in the present rather than in the past or future. This emphasis on the present is only to be expected because the young have grown up under the shadow of the bomb: the constant threat of complete annihilation. This is their glorious heritage. Can we be surprised that they should so often question the sanity of the generation that bequeathed it?

1. Which of the following features in the young is NOT mentioned?

   A) Better educated.

   B) More money and freedom.

   C) Independence.

   D) Hard work.

2. What so the young reject most?

   A) Values.

   B) The assumption of the elders.

   C) Conformity.

   D) Conventional ideas.

3. Why do the young stress on the present?

   A) They have grown up under the shadow of the bomb.

   B) They dislike the past.

   C) They think the present world is the best.

   D) They are afraid of destruction.

4. What can the old learn from the young generation?

   A) Enjoyment is not sinful.

   B) People should have more leisure time.

   C) Men might enjoy life.

   D) One should enjoy one's work.

▶**Passage two**

As citizens of advanced but vulnerable economies, we must either relentlessly increase the quality of our skills or see our standard of living erode. For the future, competition between nations will be increasingly based on technological skill. Oil and natural resources will still be important, but they no longer will determine a nation's economic strength. This will now be a matter of the way people organize them selves and the nature and quality of their work. Japan and the "new Japans" of East Asia are demonstrating this point in ways that are becoming painfully obvious to the older industrial countries.

There is simply no way to rest on our past achievements. Today's competition renders obsolete huge chunks of what we know and what forces us to innovate. For each individual. Several careers will be customary, and continuing education and retraining will be inescapable. To attain this extraordinary level of education, government, business, schools, and even individuals will turn to technology for the answer.

In industry, processing the information and designing the changes necessary to keep up with the market has meant the growing use of computers. The schools are now following close behind. Already some colleges in the United States are requiting a computer for each student. It is estimated that 500,000 computers are already in use in American high schools and elementary schools. Although there is an abysmal lack of educational software, the number of computers in schools expands rapidly.

The computer is the Proteus of machines, as it takes on a thousand forms and serves a thousand functions. But its truly revolutionary character can be seen in its interactive potential. With advanced computers, learning can be individualized and self-paced. Teachers can become more productive and the entire learning environment enriched.

It is striking how much current teaching is a product of pencil and paper technology. With the computer's capacity for simulation and diverse kinds of feedback, all sorts of new possibilities open up for the redesign of curriculums. Seymour Papert, the inventor of the computer language LOGO, believes that concepts in physics and advanced mathematics can be taught in the early grades with the use of computers.

On every-day level, word-processing significantly improves the capacity for written expression. In terms of drill and practice, self-paced computer-assisted instruction enables the student to advance rapidly — without being limited by the conflicting needs of the entire class. In short, once we learn to use this new brain outside the brain, education will never be the same.

Industry, faced with the pressures of a rapidly shifting market, is already designing new methods to retrain its workers, In the United States, a technological university has been set up to teach engineering courses by satellite. And the advances in telecommunications and computational power will dramatically expand the opportunities for national and international efforts in education and training.

Without romanticizing the machine, it is clear that computers uniquely change the potential for equipping today's citizens for unprecedented tasks of the future. Particularly in Europe and the United States, innovation will be the basis for continued prosperity. New competitors are emerging to challenge the old economic arrangements. How successfully we respond will depend on how much we invest in people and how wisely we employ the learning tools of the new technology.

1. What is the decisive factor in future competition between nations?

  A) Oil.　　　　　　　　B) Technological skill.

  C) Natural resources　　D) Education

2. The main idea of this passage is _____.

  A) Knowledge of a Computer

  B) Importance of a Computer

  C) Function of Knowledge

  D) Function of Technology

3. Why does further study become indispensable?

  A) People want to so more jobs.

  B) People want to attain this extraordinary level of education.

C）People would not rest on the past achievements.

D）What we know becomes obsolete.

4. The word "Proteus" is closest in meaning to _____.

A）flexibility　　B）diversity　　C）variety　　D）multiplicity

答案

▶**Passage one**

解析：

1. 选 D）。艰苦工作。这在第一段中第四句"青年一代受了更好的教育，有大量的钱花，有更多的自由。他们成长的很快，不那么依赖于父母，他们独立思考得更多，不盲目接受老一代的理想……。"

   A）受更好的教育；B）更多的钱和自由；C）独立性。这三项均提及到。

2. 选 C）。顺从。第二段集中讲到这一点。"因为老人们经常认为自己懂得多，理由就是他们经历得多。他们不喜欢自己的价值观受到怀疑或威胁，而这正是青年在做的。他们对老人们的设想提出疑问，打乱他们的自鸣得意。他们甚至敢于怀疑老一代创造了世界上可能最佳的社会。他们最反对的莫过于顺从。例如：他们说办公时间就是强制奴役，如果人们完全自由，绝对负责，他们的工作不会更好吗？而穿衣呢？谁说世界上所有的男人都该穿单调的灰色西装和剪成像罪犯似的短发？……。"这些词语都表示他们最反对的东西是遵从，"一致性"。所以 A）价值；B）长者的设想；D）传统习俗观念，都是具体的某一点。

3. 选 A）。他们在炸弹的阴影下成长。第三段倒数第四句起"由于年轻人是在炸弹战争的阴影下成长壮大：在不断受到全面歼灭的威胁之下，所以也只能期望他们重视目前。这是他们的光荣遗产。他们经常询问赠给他们遗产的这代人的头脑是否清醒。对此我们能表示惊讶吗？"遗产指的是第二段的种种问题所体现出来的东西，如："谁说人类的差异能通过常规政策或暴力手段予以很好的解决？为什么老一代人常用暴力来解决他们的问题？为什么他们（老一代）个人生活那么不愉快。老有负罪感？为什么老纠缠于要积聚越来越多的物质财富？……"

B）他们不喜欢过去；C）他们认为现世界是最好的；D）他们害怕破坏。

4. 选 A）。享受不是罪犯。这在第三段中间"老年人——如果他们准备承认的话——可以从他们的孩子们那里学到一两件事。他们能学的最大的课堂之一是享受不是罪犯。""享受"是人可适用于生活各个方面的原则。从工作中获得乐处，享受闲暇时间，肯定不是错误。抛弃约束限制，生活在现在而不是生活在过去肯定也不是错。

B）人们应有更多的闲暇；C）人可以享受生活；D）一个人应当享受工作。

▶Passage two

解析：

1. 选 B）。工艺技术。这在第一段就讲到"在未来，国与国之间的竞争越来越以工艺技术为基础。尽管石油和其他自然资源仍很重要，但它们不会再对一个国家的经济实力起决定性的作用。"

A）石油；C）自然资源，这两项不是决定性因素；D）教育。文内教育作为改革的一个方面，其重点是在学校内应用计算机，来改变教学质量，达到革新人才的目的。并不是直接参与竞争。可参看第2题的答案及译注。

2. 选 B）。计算机的重要性。整篇文章都显示了这一点。第三段"工业上，信息处理和制定必要的改革计划以适应市场需要意味着越来越多的使用计算机。学校紧跟工业之后……"第四段"计算机是一种变化多端，神通广大的机器，因为它显示千种图象，发挥千种功能。而它真正的革命性可在其相互作用的潜能中看出。有了先进的计算机，学习可以个别进行，速度自行规定。教师变得更有成效……"第五段"……由于利用计算机，在学校低年级就能教授物理学和高等数学概念……"最后一段画龙点睛地指出："计算机独一无二地改变着那种今天公民能担当未来空前任务的潜能……新的竞争对手正在崛起，自由的经济布局提出挑战。我们如何才能顺利的应战，取决于我们对人投资的多寡，取决于我们怎么聪慧地应用新技术的学习工具。"所以 A）计算机知识；C）知识的功能；D）技术功能，这三项只是计算机重要性中涉及到的一个方面，不能作为中心思想。

3. 选 D）。因为我们知道的一切变得陈旧。第二段头几句话"我们决不能吃老本，当今的竞争使我们的大部分知识变得陈旧，非加以革新不可。对每个人来说，他们将惯常从事某几种职业，并且非继续学习进修和从新接受训练不可……。"都说明进修学习的原因。

A）人们要做更多工作，文内没有提到；B）人们要到达非同一般的教育水平，这是目的，不是原因；C）人们不能吃老本。这话并没有完全讲清楚全部原因。

4. 选 A）。灵活多变。Proteus 一词，原意是指希腊神话中变幻无常的海神，普罗狄斯，他可以随心所欲变成各种形状。这里指灵活多变。

特训二及答案

▶Passage one

By 1950, the results of attempts to relate brain processes to mental experience appeared rather discouraging. Such variations in size, shape, chemistry, conduction speed, excitation threshold, and the like as had been demonstrated in nerve cells remained negligible in significance for any possible correlation with the manifold dimensions of mental experience.

Near the turn of the century, it had been suggested by Hering that different modes of sensation, such as pain, taste and color, might be correlated with the discharge of specific kinds of nervous energy, However, subsequently developed methods of recording and analyzing nerve potentials failed to reveal any such qualitative diversity. It was possible to demonstrate by other methods refined structural differences among neuron types; however, proof was lacking that the quality of the impulse or its conduction was influenced by these differences, which seemed instead to influence the developmental patterning of the neural circuits. Although qualitative variance among nerve rigidly disproved, the doctrine was generally abandoned in favor of the opposing view, namely, that nerve impulses are essentially homogeneous in quality and are transmitted as "common currency" throughout the nervous system. According to this theory, it is not the quality of the sensory nerve impulses that determines the diverse conscious sensations they produce, but, rather, the different areas of the brain into which they discharge, and there is some evidence for this view. In one experiment, when an electric stimulus was applied to a given sensory field of the cerebral cortex of a conscious human subject, it produced a sensation of the appropriate modality for that particular locus, that is, a visual sensation from the visual cortex, an auditory sensation from the auditory cortex, and so on. Other experiments revealed slight variations in the size, number, arrangement, and interconnection of the nerve cells, but as for as psychoneural correlations were concerned, the obvious similarities of these sensory fields to each other seemed much more remarkable than any of the minute differences.

However, cortical as diverse as those of red, black, green and white, or touch, cold, warmth, movement, pain, posture and pressure apparently may arise through activation of the same cortical areas. What seemed to remain was some kind of differential patterning effects in the brain excitation: it is the difference in the central distribution of impulses that counts. In short, Brain theory suggested a correlation between mental experience and the activity of relatively homogenous nerve-cell units conducting essentially homogeneous impulses through homogeneous cerebral tissue. To match the multiple dimensions of mental experience psychologists could only point to a limitless variation in the spatiotemporal patterning of nerve impulses.

1. Up until 1950, efforts to establish that brain processes and mental experience are related would most likely have been met with _____.

   A) vexation B) irritability

   C) discouragement D) neutrality

2. The author mentions "common currency" primarily in order to emphasize the _____.

   A) lack of differentiation among nerve impulses in human beings

   B) similarities in the views of the scientists

   C) similarity of sensations of human beings

   D) continuous passage of nerve impulses through the nervous system

3. Which of the following theories is reinforced by the depiction of the experiment in lines 16-19?

   A) Cognitive experience manifested by sensory nerve impulses are influenced by the area of the brain stimulated.

   B) Qualitative diversity in nerve potentials can now be studied more accurately.

   C) Sensory stimuli are heterogeneous and are greatly influenced by the nerve sensors they produce.

   D) Differentiation in neural modalities influences the length of nerve transmissions.

4. It can be inferred from the passage that which of the following exhibit the LEAST qualitative variation?

   A) Nerve cells.

   B) Nerve impulses.

   C) Cortical areas.

   D) Spatial patterns of nerve impulses.

▶**Passage two**

About a century ago, the Swedish physical scientist Arrhenius proposed a low of classical chemistry that relates chemical reaction rate to temperature.

According to his equation, chemical reactions are increasingly unlikely to occur as temperature approaches absolute zero, and at absolute zero, reactions stop. However, recent experiment evidence reveals that although the Arrhenius equation is generally accurate in describing the kind of chemical reaction that occurs at relatively high temperature, at temperatures closer to zero a quantum-mechanical effect known as tunneling comes into play; this effect accounts for chemical reactions that are forbidden by the principles of classical chemistry. Specifically, entire molecules can tunnel through the barriers of repulsive forces from other molecules and chemically react even though these molecules do not have sufficient energy, according to classical chemistry, to overcome the repulsive barrier.

The rate of any chemical reaction, regardless of the temperature at which it takes place, usually depends on a very important characteristic known as its activation energy. Any molecule can be imagined to reside at the bottom of a so-called potential well of energy. S chemical reaction corresponds to the transition of a molecule from the bottom of one potential well to the bottom of another. In classical chemistry, such a transition can be accomplished only by going over the potential barrier between the well, the height of which remain constant and is called the activation energy of the reaction. In tunneling, the reacting molecules tunnel from the bottom of one to the bottom of another well without having to rise over the barrier between the two wells. Recently researchers have developed the concept of tunneling temperature: the temperature below which tunneling transitions greatly outnumber Arrhenius transitions, and classical mechanics gives way to its quantum counterpart.

This tunneling phenomenon at very low temperatures suggested my hypothesis about a cold prehistory of life: formation of rather complex organic molecules in the deep cold of outer space, where temperatures usually reach only a few degrees Kelvin. Cosmic rays might trigger the synthesis of simple molecules, such as interstellar formaldehyde, in dark clouds of interstellar dust. Afterward complex organic molecules would be formed, slowly but surely, by means of tunneling. After I offered my hupothesis, Hoyle and Wickramashinghe argued that molecules of interstellar formaldehyde have indeed evolved into stable polysaccharides such as cellulose and starch. Their conclusions, although strongly disputed, have generated excitement among investigators such as myself who are proposing that the galactic clouds are the places where the prebiological evolution of compounds necessary to life occurred.

1. The author is mainly concerned with _____.

    A) describing how the principles of classical chemistry were developed

    B) initiating a debate about the kinds of chemical reaction required for the development of life

    C) explaining how current research in chemistry may be related to broader biological concerns

    D) clarifying inherent ambiguities in the laws of classical chemistry

2. In which of the following ways are the mentioned chemical reactions and tunneling reactions alike?

    A) In both, reacting molecules have to rise over the barrier between the two wells.

    B) In both types of reactions, a transition is made from the bottom of one potential well to the bottom of another.

    C) In both types of reactions, reacting molecules are able to go through the barrier between the two wells.

    D) In neither type of reaction does the rate of a chemical reaction depend on its activation energy.

3. The author's attitude toward the theory of a cold prehistory of life can best be described as _____.

    A) neutral   B) skeptical

    C) mildly positive   D) very supportive

4. Which of the following best describes the hypothesis of Hoyle and

Wickramasinghe?

A）Molecules of interstellar formaldehyde can evolve into complex organic molecules.

B）Interstellar formaldehyde can be synthesized by tunneling.

C）Cosmic rays can directly synthesize complex organic molecules.

D）The galactic clouds are the places where prebilogical evolution of compounds necessary to life occurred.

答案

▶**Passage one**

解析：

1. 选 C）。令人失望。答案见文章的第一句话"到了1950 年，大脑活动过程和精神感受有关系的实验结果看起来令人沮丧。"

   A）令人恼火；B）激怒；D）中立，均不对。

2. 选 A）。在人的神经脉冲中缺少变异（差别）。common currency 本意是一般通用。这里的上下问决定了它的含义"无变异脉冲（普通脉冲）"。第二段"虽然神经能量中的质变理论从没有受到严厉的驳斥，但这一学说被普遍放弃，而赞成其对立的观点；那就是：神经脉冲在质量上基本相似，并作为无变异脉冲（普通脉冲）经神经系统传送。"所以普通脉冲就是指神经脉冲无变异，在质量上基本相似。

   B）科学家观点上的相似性；C）人类感觉相似性；D）神经脉冲连续不断通过神经系统。这三项和 common currency 无关。

3. 选 A）。受刺激的大脑部位影响感觉神经脉冲所显示的认知感受。在第二道题译文下面"根据这一理论，不是感觉神经脉冲的质量决定它们所产生的各种有意识的感觉。而是由脉冲在大脑中释放的不同部位决定，并且有证据证明这一论点。"

   B）现在对神经潜力的质量变化可以进行更精彩的研究；C）感官刺激是异源的，并深究它们所产生的神经感觉（感受器）的影响；D）神经形态上的差异影响神经传递长度。

4. 选 B）。神经脉冲。这在第 2 题答案 A）中译注（即第二段）已有明确的答复。"神经脉冲在质量上基本相似……。"

A）神经细胞，"有可能用其他办法来显示神经细胞类型之间细微的结构差异。"；C）外皮区域（部位）；D）神经脉冲空间模式。和本文最后一句"为了和精神感受多样性吻合，心理学家只能指明神经脉冲时空模式上的无限差异。"这说明，它不是"Least qualitative variation."

▶**Passage two**

解析：

1. 选 C）。说明现在化学研究如何能和更广泛的生物学领域有关。最后一段基本上都是谈与生化的关系。"极低温时的贯穿势垒现象证明我对寒冷的史前生命的假说：在外层空间极其寒冷处，温度一般只有 K 的几度光景，有相当复杂的有机分子形成。宇宙射线可能激发诸如星际甲醛单分子在星际尘埃的乌云中综合。以后，复杂的有机分子，慢慢的，但稳定的通过贯穿势垒的方式形成。"后又有两位化学家提出"星际甲醛分子确实进化为类似纤维素和淀粉等多糖酶。"他们的结论虽有争议，却实在令人振奋，特别是文章之作者，因为他正提出"巨大的云块这些地方，发生过生命所必须的前生物进化化合物。"

A）描述经典化学定理如何发展；B）开展一场有关生命进化所需的那种化学反应的辩论；D）搞清楚经典化学定理所固有的模糊点。

2. 选 B）。两类反应中，都有一个从一个势阱底部到另一个势阱底部的跃迁。见第二段第三句起"化学反应跟分子从一个势阱的底部到另一个势阱的底部的跃迁相类似。在经典化学中，这种跃迁只有跨过两阱之间势垒才能完成。位垒之高度为常数（固定不变）。这种跃迁叫做能量活化。在贯穿势垒效应中作反应的分子从一个势阱的底部通到另一个势阱底部不需要上升跨越两阱之间的位垒。"

A）两类反应中，反应中的分子都需跨越两阱间的栏栅；C）两类反应中，反应中的分子都能穿过两阱之间的位垒；D）两类反应中，没有一种化学反应的速率取决于能量活化。这三项都不对，见上文。

3. 选 C)。有点肯定。见第 1 题答案注释译文。因为证实了作者的假设。

A）中立；B）怀疑的；D）非常支持。

4. 选 A)。星际甲醛分子可以进化到复杂的有机分子。见第 1 题 C 答案注释译文。

B）星际甲醛分子可以通过贯穿势垒方式加以综合；C）宇宙射线可以直接综合复杂的有机分子；D）大块云团是生命所需复合物前生物进化发生的地方。这三项也可从第 1 题 C 答案注译译文看出其错误点。

特训三及答案

▶Passage one

The search for latent prints is done in a systematic and intelligent manner. Investigators develop techniques to locate traces of fingerprints at a crime scene. The basic premise in searching for latent prints is to examine more carefully those areas, which would most likely be touched by persons who have been on the scene. The natural manner in which a person would use and place his hands in making an entrance or exit from a building or in handling any object is the key to the discovery of latent prints.

Where a forced entrance has been made, latent prints are likely to be found on any surface adjacent to or at that point. Any object with a smooth, non-porous surface is likely to retain latent prints if touched. Fingerprints on rough surfaces are usually of little value. If the fingermark does not disclose ridge detail when viewed under a reading glass, the chances are that its value in identification is nil when photographed. Where fingermarks are found, it will be necessary for the investigator to compare them against the ones of persons having legitimate access to the premises so that the traces might be eliminated as having evidentiary value if they prove to be from these persons. Places to search for prints on an automobile are the rear view mirror, steering wheel hub, steering column, windshield dashboard and the like.

Dusting of surface may be done with a fine brush or with an atomizer. The whit powders used are basically finely powdered white lead, talc, or chalk. Another light powder is basically Chemist's gray. A good black powder is composed of lampblack, graphite, and powdered acacia. Dragon's blood is good powder for white surface and can be fixed on paper by heating. In developing latent prints, the accepted method is to use the powder sparingly and brush lightly. Do not use powder if the fingermark is visible under oblique lighting. It can be photographed. A good policy for the novice is to experiment with his own prints on a surface similar to the one he wishes to search in order to determine the powder best suited to the surface. Fingerprints after dusting may be lifted by using fresh cellulose tape or commercially prepared material especially designed to lift and transfer dusted latent fingerprints.

In addition to latent prints, the investigator must not overlook the possibility of two other types of fingerprint traces: molded impression and visible impression. Molded impressions are formed by the pressure of the finger upon comparatively soft, pliable, or plastic surfaces producing an actual mold of the fingerprint pattern. These can be recorded by photograph without treating the surface, is usually most effective in revealing the impressions clearly. Visible impressions are formed when the finger is covered with some substance which is transferred to the surface contacted. Fingers smeared with blood, grease, dirt, paint, and the like will leave a visible impression. If these impressions are clear and sharp, they are photographed under light without ant treatment. Ordinarily, prints of this type are blurred or smeared and do not contain enough detail for identification by comparison. However, they can not be overlooked or brushed aside without first being examined carefully.

1. What is the best title for this passage?

    A) Visible impressions.   B) Moulded impressions.

    C) Fingerprints.   D) Latent fingerprints.

2. How many fingermarks are mentioned in this passage?

    A) 2.   B) 3.   C) 4.   D) 5.

3. Which type of fingerprints is most likely to retain?

    A) Latent fingerprints.

    B) Visible impressions.

    C) Moulded impressions.

    D) Clear fingerprints.

4. How many ways are there to develop fingerprints?

    A) 2.   B) 3.   C) 4.   D) 5.

▶**Passage two**

    Whenever you see an old film, even one made as little as ten years ago, you cannot help being struck by the appearance of the women taking part. Their hair-styles and make-up look dated; their skirts look either too long or too short; their general appearance is, in fact, slightly ludicrous. The men taking part in the film, on the other hand, are clearly recognizable. There is nothing about their appearance to suggest that they belong to an entirely different age.

    This illusion is created by changing fashions. Over the year, the great majority of men have successfully resisted all attempts to make them change their style of dress. The same cannot be said for women. Each year a few so-called top designers in Paris or London lay down the law and women the whole world over rush to obey. The decrees of the designers are unpredictable and dictatorial. This year, they decide in their arbitrary fashion, skirts will be short and waists will be high; zips are in and buttons are out. Next year the law is reversed and far from taking exception, no one is even mildly surprised.

    If women are mercilessly exploited year after year, they have only themselves to blame. Because they shudder at the thought of being seen in public in clothes that are out of fashion, they are annually black-mailed by the designers and the big stores. Clothes, which have been worn, only a few times have to be discarded because of the dictates of fashion. When you come to think of it, only a women is capable of standing in front of a wardrobe packed full of clothes and announcing sadly that she has nothing to wear.

Changing fashions are nothing more than the deliberate creation of waste. Many women squander vast sums of money each year to replace clothes that have hardly been worn. Women, who cannot afford to discard clothing in this way, waste hours of their time altering the dresses they have. Hem-limes are taken up or let down; waist-lines are taken in or let out; neck-lines are lowered or raised, and so on.

No one can claim that the fashion industry contributes anything really important to society. Fashion designers are rarely concerned with vital things like warmth, comfort and durability. They are only interested in outward appearance and they take advantage of the fact that women will put up with any amount of discomfort, providing they look right. There can hardly be a man who hasn't at some time in his life smiled at the sight of a woman shivering in a flimsy dress on a wintry day, or delicately picking her way through deep snow in dainty shoes.

When comparing men and women in the matter of fashion, the conclusions to be drawn are obvious. Do the constantly changing fashions of women's clothes, one wonders, reflect basic qualities of fickleness and instability? Men are too sensible to let themselves be bullied by fashion designers. Do their unchanging styles of dress reflect basic qualities of stability and reliability? That is for you to decide.

1. The main idea of this passage is _____.

　A) New fashions in clothes reflect the qualities of women

　B) New fashions in clothing are created solely for commercial exploitation of women

C) The top designers seem to have the right to creating new fashion

D) Men have the basic quality of reliability

2. Why do the general appearance of actresses look ludicrous?

A) Because they want their appearance in the fashion.

B) Because the top designers want them to follow the fashion.

C) Because the top designers want them to make fashion.

D) Because the top designers want them to lead the fashion.

3. Why are women mercilessly exploited by the fashion designers?

A) They love new fashion.

B) They love new clothes.

C) They want to look beautiful.

D) They are too vain.

4. What are fashion designers interested in?

A) Outward appearance.　　B) Comfort.

C) Beauty.　　D) Durability.

答 案

▶Passage one

解析:

1. 选 C)。指印,不管哪一种。

A) 可见压痕;B) 模性压痕;C) 潜指印,都属于指印。所以最佳的标题应是指印。

2. 选 B)。三种指印,即潜指印、模性压痕和可见压痕。

3. 选 A)。潜指印。因为潜指印隐秘,又是作案人无意中留下,不易被人发现和破坏。其价值性从文中第三段描写取潜指印可见一般。B) 和 C) 见第四段 "一定不要忽略其他两种类型的指印痕:模性压痕和可见压痕的可能性" 这说明这两种指印较少,特别是模性压痕是在相当柔软,柔韧或者塑性表面留下的,作案人一般都是小心翼翼的,不留下指印,更不太可能在这类东西上压上一个指痕。至于可见压痕,是手上沾了 "血,油脂,脏土,油漆之类物品"留下。"一般来说，这种类型的指印都是模糊不清或者是污脏难分，比较之下它们对鉴定来说，没有足够的细节证据。"

D）清楚指印，没有这个专门名称。

4. 选A）。两种。第三段第四句起"在显影指印时，公认的方法是用少许粉末，轻轻拂扫。如果指印在昏暗的灯光下可见，就可以摄影"，"指印轻扫后就用指纹胶带或商业专备材料把它们取下。这是一种专门设计用于取下和转移轻拂扫后的指印材料。"

▶**Passage two**

解析：

1. 选B）。创制新时装就是对妇女的商业性剥削。答案遍及全文。也有几段突出描述。如：第二段第四句"每年巴黎、伦敦的一些所谓高级设计师定出条条框框，全世界妇女竞相服从。设计师的条令难以预测，说一不二。"第三段"要说妇女年年被无情的剥削之事，只能怪她们自己。由于她们一想起在公共场所穿着过失的衣服就会发抖，所以他们每年都被设计师和大商店讹诈（勒索）……"第四段："许多妇女（每年）浪费大笔钱财来置换她们从未穿过的服装，时装变化就是故意创造浪费。"

A）时装反映妇女的秉性，这在最后一段结论中提及，不是中心思想；D）男人具有可靠性的基本素质，不对；C）高级设计师似乎有权创造新款式，这是作者在批评设计者。

2. 选D）。因为高级设计师请她们领导时装潮流。只是常识，设计师新颖服装的推出，首先是让演员试装——等于时装模特的效用，掀起可以领导时装的新潮流。

A）他们要打扮时髦，这只是演员的一方面；B）随大流；C）作作样子，都是不对的。

3. 选D）。他们太好虚荣。这在文章的好几段内都提到。第三段后半部分"只穿了几次的衣服就因为时尚的命令而弃之一边。当你想到只有妇女能站在堆满衣服的衣柜前，悲哀的诉说她没有衣服穿。"第四段的后半段"花不起大笔钱财买衣服的妇女会花上好几个小时把他们已有的衣服换来换去"。第五段后半部分"男人一生中经常可以看到大冬天妇女颤抖在薄薄的衣衫中，或者穿着精致的鞋在雪地上选路走，这都令他们发笑"。最后一段结论，画龙点睛的以问点明"经常不断的换时装。人们不禁要问，这是不是反映了妇女轻浮和易变的基本素质（秉性)?"

A）她们爱新时尚；B）她们爱新衣服；C）她们想瞧着美。这三项只是虚荣的部分组成。

4. 选 A）。外观。答案在第五段"没有人认为时装工业为社会作过真正的贡献。时装设计师很少关心保暖，舒服和耐穿这类紧要的事，他们只是对外观感兴趣，他们利用了妇女的心理：只要看着美，她们能忍受一切（痛苦）不舒服……。"

B）舒适；C）美，时装不一定美；D）耐穿。

特训四及答案

▶Passage one

This is supposed to be an enlightened age, but you wouldn't think of if you could heat what the average man thinks of the average woman/ Women won their independence years ago. After a long, bitter struggle, they now enjoy the same educational opportunities as men in most parts of the world. They have proved repeatedly that they are equal and often superior to men in almost every field. The hard-fought battle for recognition has been won, but it is by no means over. It is men, not women who still carry on the sex war because their attitude remains basically hostile. Even in the most progressive societies, women continue to be regarded as second-rate citizens. To hear some men talk, you'd think that women belonged to a different species!

On the surface, the comments made by men about women's abilities seem light-hearted. The same tired jokes about women drivers are repeated day in, day out. This apparent light-heartedness dose not conceal the real contempt that men feel for women. However much men sneer at women, their claims to superiority are not borne out by statistics. Let's consider the matter of driving, for instance. We all know that women cause far fewer accidents than men. They are too conscientious and responsible to drive like maniacs. But this is a minor quibble. Women have succeeded in any job you care to name. As politicians, soldiers, doctors, factory-hands, university professors, farmers, company directors, lawyers, bus-conductors, scientists and presidents of countries they have often put men to shame. And we must remember that they frequently succeed brilliantly in all these fields in addition to bearing and rearing children.

Yet men go on maintaining the fiction that there are many jobs women can't don Top-level political negotiation between countries, business and banking are almost entirely controlled by men, who jealously guard their so-called 'rights'. Even in otherwise enlightened places like Switzerland women haven't even been given the cote. This situation is preposterous! The arguments that men put forward to exclude women from these fields are all too familiar. Women, they say, are unreliable and irrational. They depend too little on cool reasoning and too much on intuition and instinct to arrive at decisions. They are not even capable of thinking clearly. Yet when women prove their abilities, men refuse to acknowledge them and give them their due. So much for a man's ability to think clearly!

The truth is that men cling to their supremacy because of their basic inferiority complex. They shun real competition. They know in their hearts that women are superior and they are afraid of being beaten at their own game. One of the most important tasks in the world is to achieve peace between the nations. You can be sure that if women were allowed to sit round the conference table, they would succeed brilliantly, as they always do, there men have failed for centuries. Some things are too important to be left to men!

1. What does the first sentence imply?

A）It is not really an enlightened age.

B）It is different from an enlightened age.

C）It is the same as an enlightened age.

D）It is like an enlightened age.

2. Why do men carry on the sex war against women?

　A）Because of their inferiority.

　B）Because they shun real competition.

　C）Because of their claim to supremacy.

　D）Because they still look down upon women.

3. The "fiction" is closest in meaning to _____.

　A）Novel　　　　　　B）Man-made idea

　C）False idea　　　　D）Story

4. What is the main argument men have raised against women?

　A）Women are lack of cold reasoning.

　B）They depend on intuition too much.

　C）They are unreliable and irrational.

　C）They are too still look down upon women.

▶**Passage two**

　The smuggler in many ways is just another international businessman and his turnover would do credit to many international corporations. His business happens to be illegal and risky, but look at the stakes involved: $5 billion worth of heroin smuggled into the United States each year, and $1.5 billion in gold passing annually along smuggling pipelines to India and Indonesia, to France and Morocco, to Brazil and Turkey. Perhaps half of all the watches made in Switzerland reach their eventual wearers by some back door. Most of this illicit trade is carried on with all the efficiency of any multinational company. Entirely legitimate businesses, such as a travel bureau or an import-export agency, are also often fronts for smuggling organizations. One of the world's largest gold smugglers also owned and operated the franchise for a leading make of British cars in a small Middle Eastern country. He made a good profit from both activities.

A smuggling syndicate operates much like any other business. The boss is really a chief executive. He makes all the plans, establishes international contacts, and thinks up the smuggling routes and method but remains aloof from actual operations. He is aided by a handful of managers looking after such specialties as financing, travel (one reason why many smuggling syndicates find it handy to have their own travel agency), the bribing of airline or customs officials, and recruitment of couriers, or mules as they are called. There may also be someone in charge of local arrangements in the countries to which the smuggled goods is going.

Another similarity between legitimate business and its illegal counterpart is price fluctuation. Just as the prices of products traded legally vary with quality and market conditions such as supply and demand, so do the prices of goods go up and down in the smuggling trade. Consider the price of drugs. Heroin and cannabis, in whatever form or by whatever name, cone in several grades, each with a going price. The wholesale price at which big dealers sell to big dealers is less than the street price. When the authorities are successful in reducing the supply buy seizures, the price of all grades rises.

1. The main idea for this passage is _____.

    A) the Comparison between Legitimate Business and Its Illegal Counterpart

    B) the similarities between Legitimate Business and Smuggling

    C) smugglers May Make Great Profit from Both Activities

    D) the Boss in Smuggling Syndicate is a Chief Executive

2. When is the price going down?

    A) The quality of the foods and market condition are not very well.

    B) The quality of goods and market condition vary.

C) Unbalance between supply and demand.

D) The price of other goods fluctuates.

3. It can be inferred that a smuggler _____.

A) may make plan and establish international contacts

B) is a real boss

C) may make money in different ways

D) may sell other goods

4. One of the best ways smugglers usually take is _____.

A) to set up multinational companies

B) to engage in illegal businesses only

C) to make legitimate businesses as fronts for smuggling organizations

D) to make good profits from both activities

答 案

▶**Passage one**

解析：

1. 选 A)。这确实不是一个启蒙时代。（1）这是第一句话语气和言词传递出来的内容。"这个时代应该是一个启蒙时期，可是假如你听到男人怎么说女人的，你就不会这么认为。"（2）整篇文章也传递了这个信息。

   B) 不同于启蒙时期；C) 这时代跟启蒙时代一样；D) 这时代像个启蒙时期。这三项都不对。

2. 选 C)。他们对至高无上权威的追求。答案在最后一段 "事实是由于男人们基本的自卑情绪，他们追求至高无上的权威。他们躲避真正的竞争。他们心里明白妇女比他们优秀，因此他们害怕在他们自己的'游戏'中失利。"

   A) 因为他们自卑；B) 因为他们躲避真正的竞争；D) 因为他们仍然轻视妇女。

3. 选 C)。错误观点。Fiction 本意为 "虚构"，此处上下文决定此意 "可是男人们继续坚持这种错误的观点：有许多工作妇女干不了，两国高级政治谈判，商业和银行几乎全部为男人们所控制，他们谨慎地保卫着他们所谓的权利。"

A）小说；D）故事，这是 fiction 的两种基本含意，这里不对；

B）人为思想。文中没有这种意义。

4. 选 C）。他们不可信，不理智。答案见第三段"他们把妇女排除这些领域之外，所提出的论点是（众所周知）老调重弹。他们说妇女不可信、不理智。在做决定时，太依赖于直觉和本能。冷静得推理太少。"

A）他们缺少冷静的推理；B）他们太依赖于直觉，这两项只是本段中用以解释"不可信，不理智的。"；D）他们太认真。这是在第二段总提到的内容"我们都知道妇女引起的交通事故比男人少得多，她们非常认真负责不会像发疯似的开车。"

▶ **Passage two**

解析：

1. 选 B）。合法商业和走私的相似性，是这篇文章的中心思想。它是通过对比方法说明这种相似性。并不是两者对比得出结论。

A）合法商业和非法商业比较，不对；C）走私者可以从两种活动中谋取利润；D）走私集团中的老板是董事长，只是对比中提到个别具体事实，不是中心思想。

2. 选 A）。货物质量和市场情况不好。第三段第二句"正如合法商业按质论价和按市场供需价一样，走私商品也是按这两者调节价格的上升和下降。"所以当质量和市场情况不好价格就跌。

B）货物质量和市场变化，这并不一定跌价，也可能上升；C）供需不平衡，并没有说明供大于求和跌价无关；D）其他商品价波动。这不一定下跌。所以 B）、C）、D）都不对。

3. 选 D）。可能会卖其他货品。题目是推断，（infer）。从第一段最后一句"世界上最大走私黄金商之买卖，可推断出走私商照样可以经营其他商品。"

A）制定计划，签定合同；B）走私商是真正的老板；C）以不同的方式赚钱，都是文章中直叙，不是推断出来的结论。

4. 选 C)。以合法商业掩护他们走私是走私商经常采用，也是最佳的方法之一。

A) 多国公司；B) 只从事非法商贸，这并不是最佳方法；D) 从两方面赚钱，并不是方法，而是有了掩护所后，多一份收入而已。

第五章　CET-4阅读真题及答案

第一节　2007年12月阅读真题及答案

Part II　Reading Comprehension（Skimming and Scanning）（15 minutes）

Directions: In this part, you will have 15 minutes to go over the passage quickly and answer the question on Answer Sheet 1.

For questions 1-7, mark

Y（*for YES*）　　　　　*if the statement agrees with the information given in the passage;*

N（*for NO*）　　　　　*if the statement contradicts the information given in the passage;*

NG（*for NOT GIVEN*）　*if the information is not given in the passage.*

For questions 8-10, complete the sentences with the information given in the passage.

Universities Branch Out

As never before in their long history, universities have become instruments of national competition as well as instruments of peace. They are the place of the scientific discoveries that move economies forward, and the primary means of educating the talent required to obtain and maintain competitive advantage. But at the same time, the opening of national borders to the flow of goods, services, information and especially people has made universities a powerful force for global integration, mutual understanding and geopolitical stability.

In response to the same forces that have driven the world economy, universities have become more self-consciously global: seeking students form around the world who represent the entire range of cultures and values, sending their own students abroad to prepare them for global careers, offering courses of study that address the challenges of an interconnected world and collaborative (合作的) research programs to advance science for the benefit of all humanity.

Of the forces shaping higher education none is more sweeping than the movement across borders. Over the past three decades the number of students leaving home each year to study abroad has grown at an annual rate of 3.9 percent, from 800,000 in 1975 to 2.5 million in 2004. Most travel from one developed nation to another, but the flow from developing to developed countries is growing rapidly. The reverse flow, from developed to developing countries, is on the rise, too. Today foreign students earn 30 percent of the doctoral degrees awarded in the United States and 38 percent of those in the United Kingdom. And the number crossing borders for undergraduate study is growing as well, to 8 percent of the undergraduates at America's best institutions and 10 percent of all undergraduates in the U. K. In the United States, 20 percent of the newly hired professors in science and engineering are foreign-born, and in China many newly hired faculty members at the top research universities received their graduate education abroad.

Universities are also encouraging students to spend some of their undergraduate years in another country. In Europe, more than 140,000 students participate in the Erasmus program each year, taking courses for credit in one of 2,200 participating institutions across the continent. And in the United States, institutions are helping place students in summer internships (实习) abroad to prepare them for global careers. Yale and Harvard have led the way, offering every undergraduate at least one international study or internship opportunity-and providing the financial resources to make it possible.

Globalization is also reshaping the way research is done. One new trend involves sourcing portions of a research program to another country. Yale professor and Howard Hughes Medical Institute investigator Tian Xu directs a research center focused on the genetics of human disease at Shanghai's Fudan University, in collaboration with faculty colleagues from both schools. The Shanghai center has 95 employees and graduate students working in a 4,300-square-meter laboratory facility. Yale faculty, postdoctors and graduate students visit regularly and attend videoconference seminars with scientists from both campuses. The arrangement benefits both countries; Xu's Yale lab is more productive, thanks to the lower costs of conducting research in china, and Chinese graduate students, postdoctors and faculty get on-the-job training from a world-class scientist and his U. S. team.

As a result of its strength in science, the United States has consistently led the world in the commercialization of major new technologies, from the mainframe computer and the integrated circuit of the 1960s to the Internet infrastructure (基础设施) and applications software of the 1990s. The link between university-based science and industrial application is often indirect but sometimes highly visible: Silicon Valley was intentionally created by Stanford University, and Route 128 outside Boston has long housed companies spun off from MIT and Harvard. Around the world, governments have encouraged copying of this model, perhaps most successfully in Cambridge, England, where Microsoft and scores of other leading software and biotechnology companies have set up shop around the university.

For all its success, the United States remains deeply hesitant about sustaining the research-university model. Most politician recognize the link between investment in science and national economic strength, but support for research funding has been unsteady. The budget of the National Institutes of Health doubled between 1998 and 2003, but has risen more slowly than inflation since then. Support for the physical sciences and engineering barely kept pace with inflation during that same period. The attempt to make up lost ground is welcome, but the nation would be better served by steady, predictable increases in science funding at the rate of long-term GDP growth, which is on the order of inflation plus 3 percent per year.

American politicians have great difficulty recognizing that admitting more foreign students can greatly promote the national interest by increasing international understanding. Adjusted for inflation, public funding for international exchanges and foreign-language study is well below the levels of 40 years ago. In the wake of September 11, changes in the visa process caused a dramatic decline in the number of foreign students seeking admission to U. S. Universities, and a corresponding surge in enrollments in Australia, Singapore and the U. K. Objections from American university and business leaders led to improvements in the process and a reversal of the decline, but the United States is still seen by many as unwelcoming to international students.

Most Americans recognize that universities contribute to the nation's well-being through their scientific research, but many fear that foreign students threaten American competitiveness by taking their knowledge and skills back home. They fail to grasp that welcoming foreign students to the United States has two important positive effects: first, the very best of them stay in the States and? like immigrants throughout history-strengthen the nation; and second, foreign students who study in the United States become ambassadors for many of its most cherished (珍视) values when they return home. Or at least they understand them better. In America as elsewhere, few instruments of foreign policy are as effective in promoting peace and stability as welcoming international university students.

1. From the first paragraph we know that present-day universities have become _____.

A) more and more research-oriented

B) in-service training organizations

C) more popularized than ever before

D) a powerful force for global integration

2. Over the past three decades, the enrollment of overseas students has increased _____.

A) by 2.5 million

B) by 800,000

C) at an annual rate of 3.9 percent

D) at an annual rate of 8 percent

3. In the United States, how many of the newly hired professors in science and engineering are foreign-born?

A) 10%.　　　　B) 20%.　　　　C) 30%.　　　　D) 38%.

4. How do Yale and Harvard prepare their undergraduates for global careers?

A) They organize a series of seminars on world economy.

B) They offer them various courses in international politics.

C) They arrange for them to participate in the Erasmus program.

D) They give them chances for international study or internship.

5. An example illustrating the general trend of universities' globalization is _____.

A) Yale's collaboration with Fudan University on genetic research

B) Yale's helping Chinese universities to launch research projects

C) Yale's students exchange program with European institutions

D) Yale's establishing branch campuses throughout the world

6. What do we learn about Silicon Valley from the passage?

A) It houses many companies spun off from MIT and Harvard.

B) It is known to be the birthplace of Microsoft Company.

C) It was intentionally created by Stanford University.

D) It is where the Internet infrastructure was built up.

7. What is said about the U. S. federal funding for research?

A) It has increased by 3 percent.

B) It has been unsteady for years.

C) It has been more than sufficient.

D) It doubled between 1998 and 2003.

8. The dramatic decline in the enrollment of foreign students in the U. S. after September 11 was caused by _____.

9. Many Americans fear that American competitiveness may be threatened by foreign students who will _____.

10. The policy of welcoming foreign students can benefit the U. S. in that the very best of them will stay and _____. (％bk％)

Part IV Reading Comprehension (Reading in Depth) (25 minutes)

Section A

Question 47 to 56 are based on the following passage.

As war spreads to many corners of the globe, children sadly have been drawn into the center of conflicts. In Afghanistan, Bosnia, and Colombia, however, groups of children have been taking part in peace education   47 . The children, after learning to resolve conflicts, took on the   48   of peacemakers. The Children's Movement for Peace in Colombia was even nominated (提名) for the Nobel Peace Prize in 1998. Groups of children   49   as peacemakers studied human rights and poverty issues in Colombia, eventually forming a group with five other schools in Bogota known as The Schools of Peace.

The classroom   50   opportunities for children to replace angry, violent behaviors with   51 , peaceful ones. It is in the classroom that caring and respect for each person empowers children to take a step   52   toward becoming peacemakers. Fortunately, educators have access to many online resources that are   53   useful when helping children along the path to peace. The Young Peacemakers Campaign. The World

Centers of Compassion for Children International call attention to children's rights and how to help the ___55___ of war. Starting a Peacemakers' Club is a praiseworthy venture for a class and one that could spread to other classrooms and ideally affect the culture of the 56 school.

A) acting   B) assuming   C) comprehensive   D) cooperative

E) entire   F) especially   G) forward   H) images

I) information   J) offers   K) projects   L) respectively

M) role   N) technology   O) victims

Section B

Passage one

Questions 57 to 61 are based on the following passage.

By almost any measure, there is a boom in Internet-based instruction. In just a few years, 34 percent of American universities have begun offering some form of distance learning (DL), and among the larger schools, it's closer to 90 percent. If you doubt the popularity of the trend, you probably haven't heard of the University of Phoenix. It grants degrees entirely on the basis of online instruction. It enrolls 90,000 students, a statistic used to support its claim to be the largest private university in the country.

While the kinds of instruction offered in these programs will differ, DL usually signifies a course in which the instructors post syllabi (课程大纲), reading assignments, and schedules on Websites, and students send in their assignments by e-mail. Generally speaking, face-to-face communication with an instructor is minimized or eliminated alto-gether.

The attraction for students might at first seem obvious. Primarily, there's the convenience promised by courses on the Net: you can do the work, as they say, in your pajamas (睡衣). But figures indicate that the reduced effort results in a reduced commitment to the course. While dropout rates for all freshmen at American universities is around 20 percent, the rate for online students is 35 percent. Students themselves seem to understand the weaknesses inherent in the setup. In a survey conducted for eCornell, the DL division of Cornell University, less than a third of the respondents expected the quality of the online course to be as good as the classroom course.

Clearly, from the schools' perspective, there's a lot of money to be saved. Although some of the more ambitious programs require new investments in severs and networks to support collaborative software, most DL courses can run on existing or minimally upgraded (升级) systems. The more students who enroll in a course but don't come to campus, the more the schools saves on keeping the lights on in the classrooms, paying doorkeepers, and maintaining parking lots. And, while there's evidence that instructors must work harder to run a DL course for a variety of reasons, they won't be paid any more, and might well be paid less.

57. What is the most striking feature of the University of Phoenix?
    A) All its courses are offered online.
    B) Its online courses are of the best quality.
    C) It boasts the largest number of students on campus.
    D) Anyone taking its online courses is sure to get a degree.

58. According to the passage, distance learning is basically characterized by _____.
    A) a considerable flexibility in its academic requirements
    B) the great diversity of students' academic backgrounds
    C) a minimum or total absence of face-to-face instruction
    D) the casual relationship between students and professors

59. Many students take Internet-based courses mainly because they can

    _____.
    A) earn their academic degrees with much less effort
    B) save a great deal on traveling and boarding expense
    C) select courses from various colleges and universities

D) work on the required courses whenever and wherever

60. What accounts for the high drop-out rates for online students?

A) There is no strict control over the academic standards of the courses.

B) The evaluation system used by online universities is inherently weak.

C) There is no mechanism to ensure that they make the required effort.

D) Lack of classroom interaction reduces the effectiveness of instruction.

61. According to the passage, universities show great enthusiasm for DL programs for the purpose of _____.

A) building up their reputation

B) cutting down on their expenses

C) upgrading their teaching facilities

D) providing convenience for students

▶ **Passage two**

Questions 62 to 66 are based on the following passage.

In this age of Internet chat, videogames and reality television, there is no shortage of mindless activities to keep a child occupied. Yet, despite the competition, my 8-year-old daughter Rebecca wants to spend her leisure time writing short stories. She wants to enter one of her stories into a writing contest, a competition she won last year.

As a writer I know about winning contests, and about losing them. I know what it is like to work hard on a story to receive a rejection slip from the publisher. I also know the pressures of trying to live up to a reputation created by previous victories. What if she doesn't win the contest again? That's the strange thing about being a parent. So many of our own past scars and dashed hopes can surface.

A revelation (启示) came last week when I asked her, "Don't you want to win again?" "No," she replied, "I just want to tell the story of an angel going to first grade."

I had just spent weeks correcting her stories as she spontaneously (自发地) told them. Telling myself that I was merely an experienced writer guiding the young writer across the hall. I offered suggestions first grade was quickly "guided" by me into the tale of a little girl with a wild imagination taking her first music lesson. I had turned her contest into my contest without even realizing it.

Staying back and giving kids space to grow is not as easy as it looks. Because I know little about farm animals who use tools or angels who go to first grade. I had to accept the fact that I was co-opting (借用) my daughter's experience.

While steeping back was difficult for me, it was certainly a good first step that I will quickly follow with more steps, putting myself far enough away to give her room but close enough to help if asked. All the while I will be reminding myself that children need room to experiment, grow and find their own voices.

62. What do we learn from the first paragraph?

    A) Children do find lots of fun in many mindless activities.

    B) Rebecca is much too occupied to enjoy her leisure time.

    C) Rebecca draws on a lot of online materials for her writing.

    D) A lot of distractions compete for children's time nowadays.

63. What did the author say about her own writing experience?

    A) She did not quire live up to her reputation as a writer.

    B) Her way to success was full of pains and frustrations.

    C) She was constantly under pressure of writing more.

    D) Most of her stories had been rejected by publishers.

64. Why did Rebecca want to enter this year's writing contest?

    A) She believed she possessed real talent for writing.

    B) She was sure of winning with her mother's help.

C) She wanted to share her stories with readers.

D) She had won a prize in the previous contest.

65. The author took great pains to refine her daughter's stories because _____.

A) she believed she had the knowledge and experience to offer guidance.

B) she did not want to disappoint Rebecca who needed her help so much

C) she wanted to help Rebecca realize her dream of becoming a writer

D) she was afraid Rebecca's imagination might run wild while writing

66. What's the author's advice for parents?

A) A writing career, though attractive, is not for every child to pursuer.

B) Children should be allowed freedom to grow through experience.

C) Parents should keep an eye on the activities their kids engage in.

D) Children should be given every chance to voice their opinions.

(%bk%)

答案

Part II Reading Comprehension (Skimming and Scanning)

1. C 2. B 3. D 4. A 5. C 6. B 7. C

8. changes in the visa process

9. take their knowledge and skills back home

10. strengthen the nation

Part IV Reading Comprehension (Reading in depth)

Section A

47. K 48. M 49. A 50. J 51. D 52. G 53. F 54. I 55. O 56. E

Section B

Passage one

57. A 58. C 59. D 60. C 61. B

Passage two

62. D   63. B   64. C   65. A   66. B

第二节　2008 年 6 月阅读真题及答案

Part II　Reading Comprehension（Skimming and Scanning）
（15 minutes）

Directions: In this part, you will have 15 minutes to go over the passage quickly and answer the question on Answer Sheet 1.

For questions 1-7, mark

Y（for YES）　　　*if the statement agrees with the information given in the passage;*

N（for NO）　　　*if the statement contradicts the information given in the passage;*

NG（for NOT GIVEN）　*if the information is not given in the passage.*

For questions 8-10, complete the sentences with the information given in the passage.

Media Selection for Advertisements

After determining the target audience for a product or service, advertising agencies must select the appropriate media for the advertisement. We discuss here the major types of media used in advertising. We focus our attention on seven types of advertising: television, newspapers, ratio, magazines, out-of-home, internet, and direct mail.

Television

Television is an attractive medium for advertising because it delivers mass audiences to advertisers. When you consider that nearly three out of four Americans have seen the game show Who Wants to Be a Millionaire? You can understand the power of television to communicate with a large audience. When advertisers create a brand, for example, they want to impress consumers with the brand and its image. Television provides an ideal vehicle for this type of communication. But television is an expensive medium, and not all advertisers can afford to use it.

Television's influence on advertising is fourfold. First, narrowcasting means that television channels are seen by an increasingly narrow segment of the audience. The Golf Channel, for instance, is watched by people who play golf, Home and Garden Television is seen by those interested in household improvement projects, thus, audiences are smaller and more homogeneous than they have been in the past. Second, there is an increase in the number of television channels available to viewers, and thus advertisers. This has also resulted in an increase in the sheer number of advertisements to which audiences are exposed. Third, digital recording devices allow audience members more control over which commercials they watch. Fourth, control over programming is being passed from the networks to local cable operators and satellite programmers.

Newspapers

After television, the medium attracting the next largest annual ad revenue is newspapers. The New York Times, which reaches a national audience, accounts for $1 billion in ad revenue annually. it has increased its national circulation by 40% and is now available for home delivery in 168 cities. Locally, newspapers are a less expensive advertising medium than television and provide a way for advertisers to communicate a longer, more detailed message to their audience than they can through television, given new production techniques, advertisements can be printed in newspapers in about 48 hours, meaning newspapers are also a quick way of getting the message out. Newspapers are often the most important form of news for a local community, and they develop a high degree of loyalty from local readers.

Radio

Advertising on radio continues to grow. Radio is often used in conjunction with outdoor billboards and the internet to reach even more customers than television. Advertisers are likely to use radio because it is a less expensive medium than television. Which means advertisers can afford to repeat their ads often. Internet companies are also turning to radio advertising. Radio provides a way for advertisers to communicate with audience members at all times of the day. Consumers listen to radio on their way to school or work, at work, on the way home, and in the evening hours.

Two major changes-satellite and Internet radio-will force radio advertisers to adapt their methods. Both of these radio forms allow listeners to rune in stations that are more distant than the local stations they could receive in the past. As a result, radio will increasingly attract target audiences who live many miles apart.

Magazines

Newsweeklies, women's titles, and business magazines have all seen increases in advertising because they attract the high-end market. Magazines are popular with advertisers because of the narrow market that they deliver. A broadcast medium such as network television attracts all types of audience members, but magazine audiences are more homogeneous. If you read Sports Illustrated. For example, you have much in common with the magazine's other readers. Advertisers see magazines as an efficient way of reaching target audience members.

Advertisers using the print media-magazines and newspapers-will need to adapt to two main changes. First, the Internet will bring larger audiences to local newspaper. These audiences will be more diverse and geographically dispersed (分散) than in the past. Second, advertisers will have to understand how to use an increasing number of magazines for their target audiences. Although some magazines will maintain national audiences, a large number of magazines will entertain narrower audiences.

Out-of-home advertising

Out-of-home advertising, also called place-based advertising, has become an increasingly effective way of reaching consumers, who are more active than ever before. Many consumers today do not sit at home and watch television. Using billboards, newsstands, and bus shelters for advertising is an effective way of reaching these on-the-go consumers. More consumers travel longer distances to and from work, which also makes out-of-home advertising effective. Technology has changed the nature of the billboard business, making it a more effective medium than in the past. Using digital printing, billboard companies can print a bill board in 2 hours, compared with 6days previously. This allows advertisers more variety in the types of messages they create because they can change their messages more quickly.

Internet

As consumers become more comfortable with online shopping, advertisers will seek to reach this market. As consumers get more of their news and in formation from the Internet, the ability of television and radio to get the word out to consumers will decrease. The challenge to Internet advertisers is to create ads that audience members remember.

Internet advertising will play a more prominent role in organizations' advertising in the near future. Internet audiences tend to be quite homogeneous, but small. Advertisers till have to adjust their methods to reach these audiences and will have to adapt their persuasive strategies to the online medium as well.

Direct mail

A final advertising medium is direct mail, which uses mailings to consumers to communicate a client's message. Direct mail includes newsletters postcards and special promotions. Direct mail

Is an effective way to build relationship with consumers. For many businesses, direct mail is the most effective form of advertising.

注意： 此部分试题请在答题卡 1 上作答。

1. Television is an attractive advertising medium in that _____.

   A) it has large audiences

   B) it appeals to housewives

   C) it helps build up a company's reputation

   D) it is affordable to most advertiser

2. With the increase in the number of TV channels _____.

   A) the cost of TV advertising has decreased

   B) the nuiflber of TV viewers has increased

   C) advertisers' interest in other media has decreased

   D) the number of TV ads people can see has increased

3. Compared with television, newspapers as an advertising medium _____.

   A) earn a larger annual ad revenue

   B) convey more detailed messages

   C) use more production techniques

   D) get messages out more effectively

4. Advertising on radio continues to grow because _____.

   A) more local radio stations have been set up

   B) modern technology makes it more entertaining

   C) it provides easy access to consumers

   D) it has been revolutionized by Internet radio.

5. Magazines are seen by advertisers as an efficient way to _____.

   A) reach target audiences

   B) modern technology makes it more entertaining

   C) appeal to educated people.

   D) convey all kinds of messages

6. Oui-of-home advertising has become more effective because _____.

   A) vbillboards can be replaced within two hours

B) consumers travel more now ever before

C) such ads have been made much more attractive

D) the pace of urban life is much faster nowadays

7. The challenge to Internet advertisers is to create ads that are _____.

A) quick to update   B) pleasant to look at

C) easy to remember   D) convenient to access

8. Internet advertisers will have to adjust their methods to reach audiences that tend to be _____.

9. Direct mail is an effective form of advertising for businesses to develop _____.

10. This passage discusses how advertisers select _____ for advertisements.

Part IV Reading Comprehension (Reading in Depth) (25 minutes)

Section A

Directions: *In this section, there is a passage with ten blanks. You are required to select one word for each blank from a list of choices given in a word bank following the passage. Read the passage through carefully before making your choices. Each choice in the bank is identified by a letter. Please mark the corresponding letter for each item on Answer Sheet 2 with a single line through the centre. You may not use any of the words in the bank more than once.*

Questions 47 to 56 are based on the following passage.

Some years ago I was offered a writing assignment that would require three months of travel through Europe. I had been abroad a couple of times, but I could hardly __47__ to know my way around the continent. Moreover, my knowledge of foreign languages was __48__ to a little college French.

I hesitated. How would I, unable to speak the language, 49 unfamiliar with locatl geography or transportation systems, set up 50 and do research? It seemed impossible, and with considerable 51 Isat down to write a letter begging off. Halfway through, a thought ran through my mind: you can't learn if you don't try. So Iaccepted the assignment.

There were some bad 52 . But by the time I had finished the trip I was an experienced traveler. And ever since, I have never hesitated to head for even the most remote of places. Without guides or even 53 bookings, confident that somehow I will manage.

The point is that the new, the different, is almost by definition 54 . But each time you try something, you learn, and as the learning piles up, the world opens to you.

I've learned to ski at 40, and flown up the Rhine River in a 55 . And I know I'll go to doing such things. It'S not because I'm braver or more daring than others. I'm not. But

I'll accept anxiety as another name for challenge and I believe I can 56 wonders.

注意：此部分试题请在答题卡 2 上作答。

A) accomplish   B) advanced   C) balloon   D) news

E) constantly   I) manufacture   J) moments   L) reduced

M) regret   F) declare   N) scary   G) interviews

O) totally   H) limited

Section B

Directions: There are 2 passages in this section. Each passage is followed by some questions or unfinished statements. For each of them there are four choices marked A), B), C) and D). You should decide on the best choice and mark the corresponding letter on Answer Sheet 2 with a single line through the centre.

▶Passage one

Question 57 to 61 are based on the following passage.

Global warming may or not be the great environmental crisis of the 21st century, but regardless of weather it is or isn't — we won't do much about it. We will argue over it and may even, as a nation, make some fairly solemn-sounding commitments to avoid it. But the more dramatic and meaningful these commitments seem, the less likely they are to be observed.

Al gore calls global warming an "inconvenient truth," as if merely recognizing it could put us on a path to a solution. But the real truth is that we don't know enough to believe global warming, and — without major technological breakthroughs — we can't do much about it.

From 2003 to 2050, the world's population is projected to grow from 6.4 billion to 9.1 billion, a 42% increase. IF energy use per person and technology remain the same, total energy use and greenhouse gas emissions (mainly, CO_2) will be 42% higher in 2050. But that's too low, because societies that grow richer use more energy. We need economic growth unless we condemn the world's poor to their present poverty and freeze everyone else's living standards. With modest growth, energy use and greenhouse emissions more than double by 2050.

No government will adopt rigid restrictions on economic growth and personal freedom (limits on electricity usage, driving and travel) that might cut back global warming. Still, politicians want to show they're "doing something." Consider the Kyoto protocol. It allowed countries that joined to punish those that didn't. But it hasn't reduced CO_2 emissions (up about 25% since 1990), and many signatories didn't adopt tough enough policies to hit their 2008-2012 targets.

The practical conclusion is that if global warming is a potential disaster, the only solution is new technology. Only an aggressive research and development program might find ways of breaking our dependence on fossil fuels or dealing with it.

The trouble with the global warming debate is that it has become a moral problem when it's really engineering one. The inconvenient truth is that if we don't solve the engineering problem, we're helpless.

57. What is said about global warming in the first paragraph?

A) It may not prove an environmental crisis at all.

B) It is an issue requiring worldwide commitments.

C) Serious steps have been taken to avoid or stop it.

D) Very little will be done to bring it under control

58. According to the author's understanding, what is Al Gore's view on global warming?

A) It is a reality both people and politicians are unawre of.

B) It is a phenomenon that causes us many inconveniences.

C) It is a problem that can be solved once it is recognized.

D) It is an area we actually have little knowledge about.

59. Greenhouse emissions will more than double by 2050 because of

_____.

A) economic growth

B) wasteful use of energy

C) the widening gap between the rich and poor

D) the rapid advances of science and technology

60. The author believes that, since the signing of the Kyoto Protocol,

_____.

A) politicians have started to do something to better the situation

B) few nations have adopted real tough measures to limit energy use

C) reductions in energy consumption have greatly cut back global warming

D) international cooperation has contributed to solving envoronmental problems

61. What is the message the author intends to convey?

A）Global warming is more of a moral issue than a practical one.

B）The ultimate solution to global warming lies in new technology.

C）The debate over global warming will lead to technological breakthroughs.

D）People have to give up certain material comforts to stop global warming.

▶Passage two

Question 62 to 66 are based on the following passage.

Someday a stranger will read your e-mail without your permission or scan the websites you've visited. Or perhaps someone will casually glance through your credit card purchases or cell phone Bills to find out your shopping preferences or calling habits.

In fact, it's likely some of these things have already happened to you. Who would watch you without your permission? It might be a spouse, a girlfriend, a marketing company, a boss, a cop or a criminal. Whoever it is, they will see you in a way you never intended to be seen-the 21st century equivalent of being caught naked.

Psychologists tell us boundaries are healthy, that it's important to reveal yourself to friends, Family and lovers in stages, at appropriate times. But few boundaries remain. The digital bread Crumbs you leave everywhere make it easy for strangers to reconstruct who you are, where you are and what you like. In some cases, a simple Google search can reveal what you think. Like it or not, increasingly we live in a world where you simply cannot keep a secret.

The key question is: Does that matter?

For many Americans, the answer apparently is "no".

When opinion polls ask Americans about privacy most say they are concerned about losing it. A survey found an overwhelming pessimism about privacy, with 60 percent of respondents saying they feel their privacy is "slipping away, and that bothers me."

But people say one thing and do another. Only a tiny fraction of Americans change any behaviors in an effort to preserve their privacy. Few people turn down a discount at tollbooths (收费站) to avoid using the EZ-Pass system that can track automobile movements. And few turn down supermarket loyalty cards, privacy economist Alessandro Acquits has run a series of tests that reveal people will surrender personal information like Social Security numbers just to get their hands on a pitiful 50-cents-off coupon.

But privacy does matter-at least sometimes. It's like health; when you have it, you don't notice it. Only when it's gone do you wish you'd done more to protect it.

62. What does the author mean by saying "the 21st century equivalent of being caught naked" (Lines 3-4, Para. 2)?

A) People's personal information is easily accessed without their knowledge.

B) In the 21st century people try every means to look into others' secrets.

C) People tend to be more frank with each other in the information age.

D) Criminals are easily caught on the spot with advanced technology.

63. What would psychologists advise on the relationships between friends?

A) Friends should open their hearts to each other.

B) Friends should always be faithful to each other.

C) There should be a distance even between friends.

D) There should be fewer disputes between friends.

64. Why does the author say "we live in a world where you simply cannot keep a secret" (Line5, Para. 3).

A) Modern society has finally evolved into an open society.

B) People leave traces around when using modern technology.

C) There are always people who are curious about others' affairs.

D) Many search engines profit by revealing people's identities.

65. What do most Americans do with regard to privacy protection?

A) They change behaviors that might disclose their identity.

B) They use various loyalty cards for business transactions.

C) They rely most and more on electronic devices.

D) They talk a lot but hardly do anything about it.

66. According to the passage, privacy is like health in that _____.

A) people will make every effort to keep it

B) its importance is rarely understood

C) is is something that can easily be lost

D) people don't cherish it until they lose it

答案

Part II Reading Comprehension (Skimming and Scanning)

1. A　2. D　3. B　4. C　5. A　6. B　7. C

8. quite homogeneous, but small

9. relationships with consumers

10. the proper media

Part IV Reading Comprehension (Reading in depth)

Section A

47. D　48. H　49. O　50. G　51. M　52. J　53. B　54. N　55. C　56. A

Section B

Passage one

57. D　58. C　59. A　60. B　61. B

Passage two

62. A　63. C　64. B　65. D　66. D